DIGITAL FACE

BOOKS BY ZELDA LEAH GATUSKIN

fiction
THE TIME DANCER
CASTLE LARK
WHERE THE SKY USED TO BE

creative non-fiction
ANCESTRAL NOTES
TIME AND TEMPERATURE

poetry
BUT WHO'S COUNTING?

art
ZELDA'S COSMIC COLORING BOOK

DIGITAL FACE

stories

Zelda Leah Gatuskin

The stories herein are works of fiction. All names, characters, places and incidents are fictitious or are used fictitiously.

Cover art by Zelda Leah Gatuskin

Printed in the United States of America
First Printing, 2016
ISBN: 978-0-938513-57-5
Library of Congress Control Number: 2015952260

AMADOR PUBLISHERS, LLC
Albuquerque, New Mexico
www.amadorbooks.com

CONTENTS

The Owl and the Pussycats 1
Handle with Care 9
Secret of The Old 16
Inside Her Eyelids 23
Digital Face 32
Tsunami 42
Bill's Aphoristic Aphrodite 54
Silver and Gold Apples 59
After Babel 93
A Man's Home Is His Castle 101
You Can Only Go Back 112

THE OWL AND THE PUSSYCATS

I met Freddy at this all-night joint called The Black Hole—not my usual sort of place. My shrink had told me I should explore my dark side, that this might help cure my Felinefilia. So there I was, all decked out in black leather and a pouty face painted on by DeRoy—the best—at Sensuale Day Spa. DeRoy also made hell out of my hair—Pebbles meets Bride of Frankenstein—which, now that I think about it, is exactly what Dr. Agatha had in mind.

I sat at a table for one with an Extra Black espresso, pretending to read a magazine about tattoos. I was paging through the back-pages ads for novelty designs when Freddy dragged a chair over and threw himself into it, bumping my knees and just about turning the table over. As I grabbed my EB and held it in the air, he put a huge paw on the table to steady it. Then he set down a drink that looked and smelled like mud, and tucked himself all in so he seemed almost normal-size.

"I'm Freddy. This is my table," he huffed.

"Oh, that's fine. You don't mind if I don't move." I tried to connect to my inner tigress, like Dr. Agatha had taught me. It was pretty easy. Freddy looked good—big and furry, like a big pussycat . . .

Oops, I wasn't supposed to be thinking like that. I had to switch mental gears fast. I have no idea what that did to my expression—getting hot for him and then thinking about kittycats and then feeling guilty—but Freddy was staring at me like he was the tiger and I was the baby bunny.

"See anything you like?" he asked, snagging the magazine. If he had any tattoos, they weren't showing.

I thought, 'What the hell. If I take him home, he's going to find out anyway,' so I said, "No, I was looking for something with a kitten, maybe a few of them, and a ball of twine, some hearts and flowers—"

Freddy laughed real hard, a good laugh that reminded me of Santa Claus, though it was more Hoo hoo hoo than Ho ho ho. Then he looked me over and said—as if he knew me already, had figured me out completely from one snarky comment—"I bet you look good in pink."

I look great in pink. Freddy liked it. He liked the kittens too. I only had half a dozen at the time. Dr. Agatha had helped me cut back.

It wasn't merely a matter of self-discipline. The doctor and I both knew better than that. I have a disease recognized by the AMA for about five years now. I am physically unable to resist kittens of ten weeks and under. Felinefilia. There's this gene that causes mammals to want to protect the young of other species, and some of us have a double dose of that, or a scrambled dose, or something. We have such an affinity for baby animals—especially kittens—that we can't see one without wanting it. Dr. Agatha tells me that, among themselves, the docs refer to my condition as Acute Cutesiness.

Only it's not that cute when the baby animals grow up and you have a house full of cats, dogs, bunnies, gerbils—I only ever succumbed to kittens, and I like cats well enough to keep them, but they don't satisfy in the same way. So I was up to my ears in cats and kittens to the point that no one would be my friend anymore, unless you count the folks at the humane association—I was starting to see them quite a lot. In fact, it was the citation from Animal Control that led me to Dr. Agatha. I didn't think I needed treatment, but it was that or pay a very big fine.

Dr. Agatha is a good person even if she does hate animals. Maybe she just puts that on as part of the treatment—that's what I tell myself. She has a way of affirming you without displaying a whisker's worth of sympathy. Tough love all the way. So she mocked me about how disgusting my house was—not cute at all—until I'd cleaned it from top to bottom. The shelters had taken all my cats and, when Dr. Agatha said I was ready, I got to start over. Two kittens. The doctor was right that I could care for my pets better and enjoy them more by not having so many. Logically, I understand that. But I went into the pet store for kitty treats—against orders, I was supposed to only buy what I could find in the supermarkets—and came home with two more kitties.

I didn't tell Dr. Agatha. I was near the end of the required counseling period and felt confident that I could manage my condition on my own. I was taking one-half the prescribed dosage of FurzReflux and figured I could keep five to ten kittens and cats without going into shock, so long as I vacuumed frequently. FurzReflux is like the medication they give alcoholics that makes them deathly ill when they drink; this stuff causes an allergic reaction to high levels of pet dander.

So I brought Freddy home to my freshly cleaned and recently redecorated house with the three sets of kittens—brand new tiny ones, perfect little scampering six-week-olds, and the original pair, almost grown. They romped over everything and shadow-boxed with Freddy while I gave him the tour. I had a 60s-pop-flower-power motif going in the living room, checkered gingham in the kitchen and dining room *à la* "Little House on the Prairie" and a classic cartoon decor in the bathrooms—only art and accessories featuring kittens, of course. My bedroom was ruffled chintz. Freddy played with the kittens while I changed into a vintage pink pajama set—complete with a short sheer robe trimmed in fake feather fluff—just so Freddy could enjoy removing it piece by piece.

It was magic. The attraction of opposites. We each found everything about the other utterly arousing. On Freddy's upper arm—one of the few parts of him where skin showed through his copious body hair—I found the tattoo. An owl framed against a full moon. It was too realistic to be either cute or creepy. The owl looked out from Freddy's arm as if it could actually see, as if it might spread its wings and come sweeping out of the flesh to take flight. But before I could ask, the arm itself swept forward to embrace me and I was out of my mind with passion. The pricking of playful little claws only added to the thrill of our love-making.

Did we wake up at noon the next day to look at one

another and wonder what ever had possessed us? Did one or the other or both regret that last espresso and the impulsive folly of our over-caffeination? No, not even for a second. I asked Freddy to move in. He agreed. He had a night job as a security guard for one of the office buildings downtown, and an apartment he shared with a couple of buddies and would be happy to leave. He liked cats. He even had a friend out in the country who would take the overflow, he told me, if I wanted to keep getting kittens. Just to prove it, when Freddy went out later to get his first load of stuff, he came back with two more pussy-babies for me. I was in heaven.

I can't think of a happier time in my life than those three years with Freddy. He slept during the day while I was at the office, then we'd spend the evening together before he went to work. With Freddy away, I'd enjoy my adorable kittens—always the right mix of them. Freddy kept me in kittens—never too many, never too old—and I kept the house in its perfect playhouse state. We were a team. Dr. Agatha was out of the picture, and I could eliminate the FurzReflux too, since I had Freddy to manage the pet situation. That owl tattoo suited him, I decided—he said the owl was his "power animal"—because he noticed everything and was very wise about it. If I so much as crinkled my nose at the litter box in the evening, the older cats would have been taken to his friends in the country by the time I came home from work the next day.

Best of all, I was being given time at work to pursue my "pet" project. Not everyone had a Freddy. And I had no delusions about "the country." I convinced my employers that a treatment that would keep kitties and puppies from maturing would be a goldmine for them, and would reduce pet over-population: More people would adopt pets if they could get a kitten or a puppy that would stay a kitten or a puppy. Plus, those pets wouldn't reproduce.

I knew the science was already out there. I'd read about the parents of a disabled daughter who asked the doctors to stunt the girl's growth with a hormone blocker so they could keep caring for her as she got older—she would be their child forever. It was a controversial treatment, to say the least. So why not back up and reformulate it for cats and dogs? I did my homework and put together a proposal for my bosses at the veterinary supply company. Not only did they go for it, they fast-tracked it. My proposal was repackaged as the Visioning Phase Report and, since my name was on it, I was put in charge. By the time the pet food companies and other manufacturers of pet products got wind of what we were doing, we already had the patents registered.

But that's all old news now. You may even have your own adorable "forever kitten" in your lap as you read this. The scientists got all the cred, of course. I was in the background, though I was included in a few interviews. And there's about thirty seconds of me, Freddy and our eight kittens in the documentary "Puppy Love" that came out last year. But the proudest day for me was when the humane association let me cut the ribbon on their new Fountain of Youth wing. I was honored by the same crew who used to fill out all those citations and harangue me about the cats.

It was the beginning of the end for me and Freddy, though. He kept taking the kittens away and bringing me new ones. I told him I didn't need new ones anymore, in fact I liked keeping the same batch. I think it made him feel like I didn't need him. He'd prowl around and hunt up all the kittens, hold them, examine them as if maybe the treatment would stop working and he could show me they were growing and needed to go. He'd bring me kittens as a gift, like in the old days, but I didn't go crazy over them the way I used to. Sometimes he'd spirit one or two away and I'd be mad at him. He became irritable, he lost weight.

The end of the end came without much fanfare. I came home from work to find Freddy's stuff cleared out. Three kittens were missing. The note on the kitchen table said, "Gotta fly, sweetheart. Feel penned in. Sick of security (and the job too, ha ha). My friends in the country say to come out—they miss seeing me. I'll drop you a line when I get settled somewhere."

So far, no line. And the kittens—I don't know, I miss seeing them grow up. I'd get a regular cat, but they're hard to find now that the unwanted pet population is way down. Someone told me that I should've had a baby with Freddy, that a baby would have solved everything. I actually had that idea myself—after the patent came through and I got another big raise—but when I mentioned it to Freddy he said no immediately, and I could tell from the look in his eyes that he meant it.

He said, "Don't do it, honeycakes. A little baby—I just don't trust myself to be a good dad. I'd hate to have to take it out to the country." Then, quick, he went and got himself some chicken nuggets—the things he liked to snack on!—and I could tell he was sublimating (I learned that from Dr. Agatha) so I didn't bring it up again.

I'd like to find a guy to have a baby with, maybe get out

of the kitten business altogether (FurzReflux is sold over-the-counter now). I've been getting out a little bit, testing the waters. But The Black Hole is out of the mix, especially after hours. I'm ready for someone who keeps the same schedule I do, so we can be real partners, not just a relay team. No more night owls for me.

HANDLE WITH CARE

Miriam, age forty, and Sarena, age fourteen, glared at each other in mute frustration. They'd been having the same argument off and on for the last three weeks. Each had exhausted her vocabulary for making her case.

Sarena had come forth with many links to articles about the popularity and safety of tattooing, down to the components in the inks and needle sterilization procedures. She had sketched out a proposed tattoo of her own design, which she was very proud of—the phrase *Handle with Care* in ornate, almost illegible script wrapping around her left upper arm. She had paraded one girlfriend after another, and some of their mothers, through the kitchen where Miriam sat from noon to 4:00 PM each day "working from home" for significantly less than was implied by the radio ads. The women, young and older, had displayed ink-adorned ankles, thighs, arms, bellies, backs, butts and boobs for Miriam's inspection. "Very artistic," she would agree, or, "Surprisingly tasteful," or sometimes, "My, how unique." But in every case her conclusion was, "Good for you, but it's not for my baby."

For her part, Miriam had tried not to fall back on the old, "Because I'm your mother and I said so" decree. She presented her own findings of conflicting research, statistics on infection and allergic reactions, and photos of badly botched art and the sad misshaping of tattoos through time. As for Sarena's motto "handle with care," Miriam was unable to hide her disdain. "Why not *Express Delivery* or *This Side Up* or *Contents may have shifted*— for god's sake, Sarena, why not a UPC code?!"

"You have no sense of humor, Mother!"

"Not about this. Not when my great-grandfather really did have a number tattooed—"

"Oh, Mother, not *that* again." And so around they went, until there was no point in even opening their mouths.

On this day, Sarena had slammed in from school, dropped her books, burst into the kitchen, and slapped her phone on the table in front of her mother.

Miriam picked it up and studied the photo. "What is that, a boob? Dear lord."

"It's a shoulder, Mother."

"Oh, well that's not so bad. But what does that say?" Miriam feigned an inability to make out the gothic lettering. "Bannister Dime? Honestly, now I've seen everything."

"Mo-ther! *Barista Diva*!"

"Oh, well, in that case."

Sarena snatched up her phone and turned toward the stairs.

"Sit down, Sarena."

Something in her mother's voice told her there were worse fates than not getting a tattoo. Sarena sat. Miriam saved her file and closed her laptop.

The women sat there and stared at each other for a long time. Until Miriam's coffee went cold. Until Sarena's screen saver switched patterns. Until the sun slanted low, and a shaft of golden light glamorized the pots and pans on the pegboard above the oven and then drowned itself in the sink.

Mother and daughter continued to sit in the deepening dusk, each racking her brain for the thing she could say that would break the standoff. Finally, Miriam spoke.

"When I was a little girl in the village, they did terrible things to us, supposedly to enhance our beauty."

It was her mother speaking, but not her mother's voice. Sarena thought she must have dozed off and was dreaming. The disembodied voice in the dark seemed to come from beyond the walls of the house. Either Sarena was dreaming or her mother was.

"Disks in our lower lips the size of saucers, plugs in our earlobes, brass rings to lengthen our necks. They'd take stinging insects, sometimes thorns from a poisonous plant, and apply them all around the waist or upper arm or lower leg in a pattern of wounds that would become infected and then heal—hopefully—into raised, whitened welts, and that would be our decoration. If we did not get sick and die, it would be a sign of our purity and heartiness."

"Mom?" Sarena got up and turned on the light. Her mother was still a tired-looking white woman with blond hair showing dark roots. Her neck, earlobes and lips were normal-sized and undecorated, her upper arms smooth and pale as peeled potatoes. Miriam blinked in the sudden light. For the first time in weeks, Sarena's tone softened. "You were dreaming, Mom, and talking in your sleep."

"No, I don't think I was dreaming. I remember what I

said. I was describing my own memories."

"Really, Mother? A past life?" The familiar scorn came roaring back.

"Past lives. The things I described could not possibly have all been experienced by the same person. Those traditions of body ornament come from all different places."

"Oh, so we're talking about *lots* of past lives. Yeah, that explains everything. Excuse me."

Sarena went upstairs. Miriam cleaned up her work space and set the table for dinner.

When Mark came home, the three ate in silence. Then Sarena showed her father the photo of her friend's shoulder.

"What does that say?" he puzzled, turning the screen one way and another. "8 Artists Dire?"

"Christ!" Sarena snatched the device from his hands and stormed up to her room.

Miriam told Mark about her past lives vision while they were getting ready for bed. She tried not to make too much of it, though it had been weighing on her mind.

"Are you sure you were flashing back to past lives and not just your childhood looking at *National Geographic*?" Mark laughed.

"Yeah, that's probably it." Miriam laughed with him.

Sarena came home the next day to find her mother sunbathing on the little back patio.

Mark found her preparing dinner in a colorful new dashiki.

In the weeks that followed Miriam had her hair cut short enough to get rid of the bad blond dye job. Short, dark curls hugged her scalp. She had her ears pierced and bought big hoop earrings. Her husband and daughter humored her, but they tried not to let conversation drift to the "African past lives" topic. The talk made Miriam sound like a kook, whereas the new look was actually rather cute.

The business of Sarena's tattoo seemed to have been settled. Miriam had outplayed her daughter, and all references to the tattoo suddenly ceased. The fact that her mother was newly cool made Sarena not want to be cool. She would have liked to become invisible. Their role reversal was complete: The mother, who ought to have been modest and inconsequential, had stolen the spotlight from the daughter, who was now consigned to looking on disapprovingly from the wings. Sarena's life went from numbingly dull to surreal. She dreaded what she might discover her mother wearing or doing next. One day she came home to find Miriam playing a wooden drum, the next week she was deep-frying crickets.

On her fifteenth birthday Sarena discovered a card on her dresser. The envelope contained two hundred dollars in cash and the battered permission slip from the tattoo parlor finally signed, by *both* her parents.

"Damn, that past-life African sex must be really good," Sarena told the permission slip. She trotted down the stairs happily, then stopped in horror. Her father was sitting at the kitchen table across from her mother with the cute new look. He was unusually cheery as he ate his oatmeal and scrolled through the news—dressed in a colorful dashiki and crown-shaped cloth cap.

"What is wrong with you two?!" Sarena wailed, making a u-turn. A few drawer-slamming minutes later, she was descending again, backpack in hand, and heading for the front door with steely calm.

"I'll be at Jenny's!"

Sarena settled into the padded chair and braced herself for the artist's needle. Her girlfriend Jenny sat supportively nearby, and Jenny's mother waited patiently on one of the benches out under the portale. Bethany approached with her needle and asked "Are you sure?" one last time before tackling Sarena's young flesh.

It hurt more than Sarena expected. She felt dizzy and closed her eyes. Then the vision came to her: An old woman holds a red ant pinched between her fingers and lowers it toward Sarena's—or someone's—brown arm. It bites! The pain! It must be her own arm. The ant is being lifted and lowered to her arm again . . .

"I'm sorry, but you're in way too much distress. I can't do this." Bethany put down the needle and draped a cloth on Sarena's arm, which had been barely poked, and another on her forehead.

Sarena sat up with a start and felt the tears spill down her cheeks. She caught the cool cloth and wiped her face with it, her mind racing while Bethany, the tattoo parlor manager, Jenny and Jenny's mom hovered over her nervously.

"I'm okay, really." She shook her hair back and met Bethany's eyes. "I was trying to chill, and I guess I fell asleep, 'cause I had a super scary dream. I'll be okay, really. How far did you get?"

Bethany lifted the cloth. There was one dot of black ink on Sarena's arm.

"Oh, great, I got a period."

Everyone cracked up at that, but the manager refused to let Bethany proceed. Sarena declined a refund. She took the receipt and asked Bethany if it would be okay to change the design.

"Well, I suppose," the artist teased, "as long as it doesn't mess up what I did today—that's some of my best work right there." Sarena turned beet red, and the manager gave Bethany a dirty look. Bethany put an arm around Sarena's shoulder and walked her out. "No problem, really. Here's my card. Send me a sketch, okay? See you real soon."

"Well?" Mark called up the stairs. This was the day on which Sarena was allowed to remove the gauze from her tattoo. The kitchen calendar bore witness to the agonizing countdown. "Are you happy with it?" It was impossible to tell if her exclamations were of delight or distress.

"Oh, yes! Wait 'til you see—" A few minutes later Sarena glided down the stairs. "I really love it. Look."

"Miriam, look," Mark urged.

Miriam turned from the sink and dropped her jaw at the sight of Sarena in a bright dashiki and matching turban.

Smiling proudly, Sarena raised her loose sleeve and thrust out her arm to show her parents. In flowing but perfectly legible script that circled her slim arm twice midway between elbow and shoulder were the words: *My Mother was an African Princess.*

SECRET OF THE OLD

Everyone is born knowing the secret of The Old, my great-grandmother told me, and all of the other great secrets of life and death. But, being babies, the information is of no use, or even recognized, so we quickly forget and then have to learn it all again. It was very unusual, she told me, for me, a girl just turned six, to retain any part of that knowledge. Because that made me special, she told me, she would entrust me with all of the rest of it, as much as she had so far remembered. Then it would be up to me to decide what to do with it, or about it, but I could be certain that if I told anyone younger than she, they would say I was very imaginative—and if anyone old, like her, tried to back me up, they would say he or she was senile.

And so Granny Mimmi told an outrageous story, me loving every minute of it and absolutely convinced of its truth. Then I practiced it to myself night after night until it seemed much more like a made-up tale and much less like truth. My great-grandmother never spoke of it again and hardly remembered who I was on her next visit. And her next visit after that didn't happen because she had died.

There were other old people in my life, Mimmi and Grampa, my mother's parents, and Ima and Aba, my father's parents. My Mimmi was Granny Mimmi's youngest child and the oldest of all those grandparents. Being well past that age now myself, I can tell you it is not so very old, not old enough to have started remembering the secret or to recognize the truth of it when blurted from the mouth of a six-year-old. So, as opportunity presented itself, and I found myself alone with one and then another of these elders, and asked the same questions that I had asked of Granny Mimmi on my sixth birthday, I did not receive any response that remotely affirmed the story I had been telling to myself every night since.

What I had said to Granny Mimmi was this: "Is it really you in there?" And then, when the very bent and wrinkled woman pursed her lips and crinkled her brow, making her look even more furrowed and strange, I half-cried: "Where is my Granny?!"

Because I was upset, she could not be silent. She said, "Do not be afraid, child, it is all so very natural. You mustn't be afraid of The Old. I love you very much."

The story she told me rang truer and truer with every word, as though I was actually remembering it, not hearing it for the first time. And indeed I felt very loved.

But a few months later when I said to Granny Mimmi's daughter, my Mimmi, "Is it really you in there?" Mimmi thought I was commenting on her new hairdo and made much of laughing and telling me how clever I was, though I could tell she was really annoyed and entirely Mimmi in every way.

I did not attempt a similar interview with Grampa because

he seemed quite himself as well, and I was afraid that if he and Mimmi compared notes they would think I was becoming a rude child and tell my mother.

When the weather warmed up, Ima and Aba arrived for their annual visit. They did not appear greatly changed, but Aba complained about pain in his hip and refused several foods he had formerly enjoyed, saying they disagreed with him now. I had him to myself that first Saturday of their stay, when the others had gone to Temple and left me home with him, because I complained of a sore throat. Aba didn't go to Temple, that was nothing new. But when I asked him to read a comic book with me, and he folded his arms and said, "No lap!" I felt that something had turned inside him.

"Is it really you in there?" I demanded, planting myself in front of his knees.

He looked stricken at first and then broke into a wide smile that could only belong to Aba. "You little rapscallion," he said, opening his arms, "I only wanted you to keep that cold to yourself!"

I hopped into his lap and said, "I don't have a cold! I only wanted to stay home with you!"

After that I did not ask any more old people about the secret, because I didn't want to upset them or hurt their feelings. I began to read chapter books and stopped telling myself Granny Mimmi's story every night. I forgot about it for long stretches, and when I remembered, my memory was vague. Eventually I began to grow breasts and go through other bodily changes that made me look in the mirror and ask myself: "Is it really you in there?"

One day the answer came back, "No, of course not, I'm not that little girl anymore at all." And I forgot the secret completely.

Now I am old, and very close to being The Old, which is very close to death. I have great-grandchildren of my own. They are dear things, like any children. Some are very affectionate towards me and some cry in fear because I look a lot like the witches in their storybooks, creased and crooked as I am. None of them are special in the way I was. None of them have an inkling left of the knowledge that came with them from the womb, which is probably just as well. For me it was only like the impression of a wrinkle in the pillowcase that is left on the cheek after a night's sleep. I had slumbered more deeply, with less disturbance, and the mark was deeper and took longer to fade, but inevitably it did and all was forgotten until very recently.

I had a life, not exceptionally successful, but not without achievement. A full life—here is the multitude of offspring to prove it, along with a shelf containing the score of books I have written, mostly outlandish stories of the sort that children love. Now I'm going to write one more, only this one will be true, every part of it, it won't be for children, and it won't actually be written by that author whose name you see at the top of the page.

I have written "I" as though I were she—the author, the six-year-old, and the young woman and mother in between. But the secret of The Old, which is what I am now, and what Granny Mimmi was when she told it to me, is that The Old is not any one person. I am The Old almost completely, but not so much that I can't write this down.

I wonder how I can tell this so my readers will follow the difference between the I who was in this body for most of her life and the I who is The Old. The I who became a writer says to switch to the third person. Her name is at the top of the page. As a child she was called Sheri. The secret of The Old that Granny Mimmi told Sheri was not really forgotten but only buried. It came rushing back to Sheri on her seventy-fifth birthday, when she felt rotten and looked in the mirror at her white hair and splotchy skin and asked, "Is that really you in there?"

The answer that came back from decades past was, "Don't be afraid, child, it's all so very natural." Child? And suddenly the memory was back, and Sheri recognized The Old looking back at her from the mirror. Without fear Sheri immediately surrendered as much of herself as she could currently spare to The Old, in order to know it better, sooner, while she still had strength to pen this account.

Sheri is well aware that heads are shaking now and words like "senility" and "dementia" are approaching tongue-tips. Some readers are putting the pages aside in disappointment. Not what they expected, not up to the author's usual level of excellence. What can she do? The Old is not accustomed to such activities and is not happy at this little trick that has been played. The Old has a secret and Sheri is about to tell it. There is tremendous interference from The Old, from the spasms in Sheri's decrepit hand, and from a large, worried family that won't leave her alone. Her only hope of getting this down, she realizes, is to think back to that story her great-grandmother told her on her sixth birthday and which she recited back to herself night after night—to let the words flow onto the paper in exactly the same order, like a song one never thinks about but is able to sing all the way through if only the first few notes can be recalled.

This will be Granny Mimmi's story, The Secret of The Old, exactly the way Sheri locked it into her memory in the nights that followed its telling. The writer says to go back to first person now, and let the "I" be Granny Mimmi and The Old together, and with any luck the song will come out like it should.

"Do not be afraid, child, it is all so very natural. You mustn't be afraid of The Old. I love you very much . . ."

I am not the person who Granny Mimmi was. A little bit of her is here but less and less all the time. When there is none left, and the old woman's body weakens and dies, I will withdraw but I will still exist. The Old is forever, as long as human history, as far as the future ever is. I am singular and do not need a body. I am neither man nor woman. People like you, and Granny Mimmi when she was young, see yourselves as many unique individuals. I see you people as all one, a being I call Humanity, and I interact with you all as one, by being your Old. The old ones among you let me in, little by little, when they grow tired of being. They let me in or I do not go. I never go where I am not wanted. Those who let me in gradually learn to know me, to know the secret, and they feel reassured, and they let me do more of the work for them, and through them I find many ways to communicate to Humanity.

"You see, my child, the language of Humanity is Life, and only by joining with your old ones can I interact with your species. To you I am The Old but not to myself. I do not consider myself old because I am not governed by time.

"It is not clear to me why humans come into the world aware of me and aware that other-than-human beings exist, until their busy minds drive the memories away. These are things even I don't know. I can only suppose that as you are to me—that is, of limited awareness by comparison—I am to another, and on and on."

Right at this point—she who is writing had almost forgotten this—Granny Mimmi broke the spell and said something Sheri didn't understand but that made her giggle.

"There's that expression, *Turtles all the way down*. But really, it's turtles all the way *up*."

They laughed together, and the spell was broken. After a time, all Sheri could remember was the turtles.

Like a turtle, this leathery hand has slowed so that she who is writing will not remember from one word to the next for very much longer. The Old is here to help, but The Old does not willingly write its thoughts. If you want to know The Old before your natural time, you must work at remembering all that you knew while in the womb. But don't worry if you can't manage. Live long enough, and The Old will come to you. It's something to look forward to.

INSIDE HER EYELIDS

Adrienne had spent the past twenty-seven years painting what she saw on the inside of her eyelids. While other artists shlepped around with their *plein air* paint kits or hired in models, Adrienne merely pressed the heels of her hands to her eye sockets and observed the firings of her rods and cones. Not that she didn't labor over production. By now she had explored every conceivable medium and its capacity to convey the dense, mildly fluorescent gradations of color that fill the field of vision we normally think of as no-vision. To emulate the entirety of the experience, of seeing nothing-but-that, Adrienne's canvases became increasingly large. They gained critical approval with her "Eyescapes" exhibition at the Whitney, and sold well thereafter. Custom wall-sized works were commissioned. Her "Sunbathing" motif in rich orangy reds, the "Dark Room" paintings (for bedrooms, naturally) and the diverse "Afterimage" series were especially popular.

With her financial needs met, Adrienne was able to establish a traditional work week routine divided equally between staring into her eyelids and rolling paint onto vast canvases. She permitted herself several weeks per year of vacation and travel, during which she got away from painting altogether—and lately found she didn't even miss it. Certainly she liked her work, but she no longer felt driven by it in the way she had when she was younger and still experimenting. She actually listened to what was on the radio now as she spread her colors, eyes and hands communicating via pathways that circumvented conscious thought. As soon as the program switched from music to news, she'd roller her way to a stopping point and start cleaning up—whereas she used to set an alarm for herself, and even then Jeff would sometimes have to call over to remind her of their evening engagements.

Adrienne and her life partner Jeff enjoyed going out. Her prestige and his affability ensured many invitations to lively evenings of parties, concerts and theater. She preferred to stay away from art receptions, but did attend the occasional wine-and-cheese soirée out of friendship, or simply in homage to the dues she'd paid. It was a little of both tonight. The artist was their broker's niece. Plus, Adrienne needed to contemplate her career goals. How better to come to a decision about the future than to remind oneself of the past?

"Remember when we used to pore over the weekly arts listings to pick out the receptions with the best food?" Adrienne asked Jeff, turning her face to him in the darkened interior of the limo, her cheek against the soft leather.

"Yes," Jeff said with a smile, turning to her in the same way. "Veggies, ranch dip, Melba toast, Gouda, petit fours and wine—"

"Preferably champagne!"

"—a perfectly balanced diet."

"If you can fill that tiny plate four times before you get kicked out."

They shared a laugh. This was the first they'd spoken since leaving the house, except for peeved exclamations about the traffic jam in which they'd been stuck for fifteen minutes. On both their minds was the offer Adrienne had received that morning from media mogul Scoop VanPeters. He was offering big money for the rights to use her images in digital flat screen art and home projection products. From first mention, it had the stink of total sell-out. But, here at day's end, Adrienne had to admit to liking the smell of money, just as she liked the aroma of fine leather upholstery.

"My paintings are of light, essentially," she told Jeff now, as if they'd been carrying on this conversation all day, when in fact they had done everything to avoid it. "The perception of light—which is all that seeing is—in the absence of light. So the idea of projecting them on a screen *in* light is kind of appealing, almost like a natural evolution of the form. Conceptual at another level."

"Huh," Jeff answered, noncommital. He liked money as much as the next guy, but they had plenty now. It wasn't like he would ever quit his job, which was a plum—menswear buyer for Cecil & Sons department stores.

"And it would make my art more accessible. Now, everyone will be able to afford an Adrienne," Adrienne continued, feeling magnanimous.

"Everyone who can afford a wall-size TV," Jeff corrected her.

"Which is way more than can afford an original Adrienne," she shot back. "Don't you think it's kind of cool that more people can have my art in their homes, without me having to paint more? All I have to do is turn over my portfolio and cash the check—I'd never have to paint another canvas—"

She stopped then, eyes widening. The statement took them both by surprise. Jeff looked concerned.

"I didn't realize this was about whether you would keep painting or not. If the thing takes off, won't VanPeters want more?"

"I have zillions of those images, Jeff. He only asked for two dozen to start. If he gets through two hundred, the public will be as tapped out as I am."

"I didn't realize—"

"No, I didn't either until this offer, until I started thinking. I guess I feel like I've done every variation, it's just spec work now. The clients pick 'em out like they're picking out paint chips. They might as well put in a screen, buy a disk, and then change the channel whenever they want. A mural without the mess."

"You don't want to paint anymore?" Jeff could see Adrienne's point, but he liked her rigid schedule in the studio—liked that she worked when he worked, and then they went out to play together. A small staff took care of their home. What would she do if she didn't paint?

Adrienne couldn't say. It scared her a little. She shook her head, leaned back and closed her eyes. *Limo Cruising City Streets: horizontal streaks of green-blue, bursts of yellow*... These compositions came unbidden and almost unobserved. But then something very peculiar— A small figure in the lower left was tip-toeing along the bottom of her visual field. Adrienne opened her eyes, then squeezed them shut again. He was still there, as if waiting for her. He seemed to motion to her— Adrienne sat upright with a start and blinked hard several times.

"What's wrong?"

"I'm hallucinating, but only when I close my eyes. I guess it was bound to happen. There's a little man inside my eyelids."

"Okay, babe, maybe it is time for you to paint something different." Jeff reached for her hand. He had no attachment to the eyelid paintings except for the security they provided. The deal with VanPeters didn't thrill him, he thought it cheapened Adrienne's work. But if she was burning out, that was different—he could see the beauty of it. "You go ahead and do what you need to do."

"I knew you'd understand," she said, intertwining her fingers with his. Adrienne blinked back tears of emotion for something that had been terribly, secretly, pent up. "The fact is, I've been thinking about hanging up the old paint roller for a while now."

"Really?"

"Not actively, like I had to get out right away, but in the back of my mind. I guess it was creeping up on me." Saying that, Adrienne experimentally shut and opened her eyes. Even in that instant she perceived the little man tip-toeing across her eyelids. How long had he been there, also on the edge of consciousness? Or was he the very reason she wanted to stop painting?

"I think it's perfectly fine that you do something else."

Jeff's reassurance put an end to the conversation. The gallery was just ahead. Adrienne did not mention the little man behind her eyelids again. She turned to the window to enjoy the visual detail of an eyes-open world, feeling she had achieved a nicely balanced life between inside and outside her eyelids, and wondering vaguely why she should have to go mad now, on the eve of her retirement.

Adrienne taught herself to fall asleep with her eyes open. She could lie in the darkened room and feel the shadowy shapes the way she did when her eyes were closed, only the little man wasn't there. Jeff would sometimes notice her staring up at the ceiling fan and talk to her. She wouldn't answer. Later he would tell her she'd been asleep with her eyes open and she'd say, yes, she must've been. After ten days of insomnia she could really do it.

Once Adrienne was asleep, though, her eyes would close, and sometimes in the night her dreams would transition to "the nasty gremlin and his obscene gestures," as she came to think of him. She would wake with a start. In truth, the gestures were no more than an invitation to follow, or to look more closely, but Adrienne was too perturbed by the hallucination to perceive any such nuance. Jeff attributed her agitation to artistic mania, since Adrienne was suddenly spending many hours in the studio, more than had been her habit in recent years.

The studio was Adrienne's escape. She occupied her time there painting complex floral still-lifes with fine brushes, seeking to depict every perceptible detail with perfect precision. Anything to avoid the horrible little man behind her eyelids. She thought that if she could fill up her visual field the way she had once emptied it, she could crowd out her secret, terrifying hallucination.

After eight months of this, exhaustion set in. The brush

strokes of Adrienne's purple dahlias began to vibrate off the canvas, and the living flowers on a stand nearby looked almost as blurry. Casting aside her palette, Adrienne collapsed into the old couch and closed her eyes.

"Go for it," she told the demon, who appeared as always in the lower left of her dark plane and tip-toed across to the right, motioning conspiratorially for her to follow. He marched and marched, silhouetted against a background she had painted many times, one that now seemed to roll along endlessly. He tip-toed and tip-toed but never went out of view, like a mime only pretending forward movement. And then he stopped, looked directly at her—sort of up and into her eyes from below, yet from within, she would think later—at any rate, getting her complete attention.

And then the little man peeled back something like tape, or a blindfold—yes, as if she had been blindfolded all this time—and revealed a world unlike anything she had ever seen or imagined. Nothing from books or stage or film or games or her own fantasies could possibly compare. She lay back with her eyes closed, looking around at everything, applying all her skills of observation, visual analysis, and memory.

□ □ □

"Quite remarkable, Adrienne, that you could have two such successful careers. The first as a painter of large abstract works and now as writer-producer of several blockbuster sci-fi series. How did you manage to make that transition? And where do your ideas come from?"

The interviewer leaned in admiringly. A green light blinked on the camera in Adrienne's face. Adrienne leaned toward the light and smiled, prepared to share her secret.

"It wasn't a transition at all, Teddy. I'm still doing what I always did—portraying what I see on the inside of my eyelids."

"Now, explain that, Adrienne. You've been quoted before as saying that, but what you really mean is that you use your imagination, right?"

"Well, possibly it is my imagination making images out of whatever it is that's there when I close my eyes. Afterimages, neurons firing— You'd think I'd've looked into the biology of it by now, but I confess I never did. I only know that when our lids close, our eyes are still *on*." Adrienne smiled brightly at the green light. "Maybe everyone out there should close *their* eyes for a minute and see what they see." The green light blinked to red.

"Oh, hoho, hahah," Teddy laughed, while a producer's tirade scalded his earpiece. "We don't want to tell our *viewing* audience to *close their eyes*! In fact, how about we go to a break? Now keep your eyes *open*, everyone, and *watch* these important messages from our *sponsors*!"

Watching the monitor in the greenroom, Jeff pulled his phone from his pocket and caught the agent's call on the first tone. "Brucey baby! . . . Yeah yeah yeah . . . Not funny? I think it's a hoot! . . . Look, we don't need the damn exposure. Adrienne's solid gold. She can say any damn thing she wants . . ."

Bruce had a lot to say to that. Jeff settled back to listen. It wasn't his gig, after all. It was Adrienne's, and sometimes it seemed to weigh heavy on her. He just wanted her to be happy—his darling genius.

A minute later, Teddy was back on the air, but Adrienne was not sitting across from him. She was slouching dejectedly into the greenroom. Jeff sat up and reached out a hand to her, mouthing the words, "It's Bruce," while he held the phone to his ear. Adrienne came to him and snuggled, comforted.

"Okay, okay," Jeff said, squeezing Adrienne to him. He held the phone so they could all three hear each other. "What do you say, guys, maybe just radio from now on?"

"Let me see what I can do," Bruce grumbled.

Adrienne wiped away a tear. "Thank you, Bruce, I'm so sorry about this. Maybe you should let Jeff do the TV spots. He is the most charming and well-dressed man in the world—no, in the universe. And *you* are the most kind and clever," she added affectionately. Her affliction was becoming more acute, but she felt lucky to have these two on her side.

"Make that all the universes."

DIGITAL FACE

"The pores! You must get rid of the pores!" Lillith insisted, leaping from her high swivel chair. She paced the capacious dressing room energetically. "I don't want pores or zits or spots or even these dots over the 'i's in my name! I don't like the 'l's either—they look like hairs. I don't want any hairs, or follicles. Ugh. *Follicle*. Horrible word. Double 'l' like Lillith. I need a new name. Something with no 'l's or 'i's. Only round letters, shapely letters—

"Where was I?"

"You don't want pores, L . . ."

"Don't say it!"

". . . ove." Gogo Forritt, the make-up artist, sat pensively on his own high swivel chair, his airbrush in hand. "That is why I am here. We paint them out. The camera never sees the pores."

"I see them. In the mirror. Everyone who sees me in person sees."

"But, Madame—"

"Hush! Listen to me, Gogo. The make-up is perfect, but it can't hide everything. I need a filter, darling, a digital cover-up. I was all set to have my pores filled at that new clinic in St. Tropez when those women died. The pores must breathe. Who knew?"

Gogo arched his eyebrows ironically, raised his left hand from the elbow and wiggled his fingers. "I did."

"Smarty pants. Good thing I didn't have a chance to not take your advice." Lillith slowed her pacing to pinch his arm. "I was even going to have my nostrils shrunk, but I suspect you are right on that score too. The first woman to be hospitalized had shrunk her nostrils *and* sealed her pores, and I heard that she'd also had a mouth tuck to make it like a Cupie doll mouth. Have you seen that? It's *so* cute! But I just don't think that the surgical approach is worth it."

"Well, obviously—" Gogo puffed up for a short I-told-you-so" speech, but his employer wasn't finished. Lillith silenced him with a sharp look and continued:

"Because now we learn that there is *another* downside of the pore eradication procedure—"

"Besides dying?"

"On *top* of dying! So I've been told. I heard that those women looked *awful* when they died. You'd think they'd be already ready for viewing, if you know what I mean—all botoxed up and well preserved—but what I *heard* is that the mortician couldn't do a *thing* with them. Had to have a *closed casket*. At least that's what I heard. So scratch that. The damn pores have got to keep working. I just don't want anyone to see them. I want some kind of soft focus, like I get on my show."

The media sensation formerly known as Lillith slid back into her chair and waited for Gogo, who had never failed to fulfill her cosmetic demands, to produce a miracle.

"You've given this a great deal of thought," Gogo replied to buy time.

"I have. And now it's your turn, darling. I'm going to wear a veil over my face in public until you've found a way to make the pores disappear. You'll be rich if you succeed, because I'll pay you well for your system, *plus* I'll pay you *incredibly* well not to tell anyone. I will be the first and *only* poreless-*in-person* personality. I want a smooth, poreless, perfect, soft-focus face wherever I am! Have you got that, Gogo?"

"Well, I'm not sure—"

"I might take to wearing veils, you know. I wouldn't need a makeup artist at all. I could trade you in for a veil person."

"I doubt you would be comfortable in a veil, Lillith, and think of the gossip."

"Not Lillith! I'm changing it! And when I finally lift my veil, I'll have a new perfect face, too. We'll be the talk of the town. What do you say?"

Gogo put aside the airbrush and finished off Lillith's face with the soft tip of a mink smoothing tool. He'd ask his nephew, who knew something about holographic animation.

"Your wish is my command. One digital face coming right up."

□ □ □

"What have you decided to call yourself, my precious?" Gogo asked, lifting his client's elegant taupe veil with the reverence of a groom for his bride. He hadn't seen her in months. Like a besotted groom, he was struck anew by her beauty, and he heard his nephew's low whistle behind him as Edgar got his first close look at one of the biggest stars of his lifetime.

"I don't know what we're doing here," the young man exclaimed adoringly. "She's gorgeous just the way she is. Doesn't even need makeup, let alone a digital face!"

Gogo rolled his eyes and made the introductions. "My nephew, Edgar. He mostly lives inside a computer game. Not used to seeing live women."

"He's charming! I'm charmed. And you may call me Bocou," she extended a gloved hand to each of the men and squeezed their hands warmly. "That's B-O-C-O-U, like *beaucoup* in French but without the awful "p" or "e" or "a"—so common. It means "much"—bounteous. I put on a few pounds while hiding out at the chalet. I think it's smoothing, don't you?" The new Bocou released the men and slid her hand along her cheek.

"You look like a billion bucks," Gogo agreed, growing concerned that he and Edgar had just wasted two months of full-time effort on another "nevermind" project. Always a risk when catering to the rich.

Bocou allayed his concerns, "I wanted to look my very best for the portrait, darlings. This is going to be the foundation of my digital face for the foreseeable future. Once you have absolutely every angle you need, I promise to completely let myself go!"

Bocou chortled and made herself comfortable in Gogo's Chicago studio. She dropped her designer handbag on the Victorian fainting couch, slid out of her heavy mink, and carefully removed the pillbox hat with its filmy veil. Her face was scrubbed clean, make-up free, tanned, and beautifully textured with small laugh lines accumulated over sixty years of comfortable living. She hopped into the swivel chair while Gogo prepared his tools and Edgar set up his cameras and lighting equipment.

"Now, darling, explain how you're going to do it, and I shall be silent for the duration." Bocou set her mouth into a gentle pout, softly lowered her lids, and lifted her chin exactly as Gogo required.

"She means you," Gogo told Edgar, priming Bocou's flesh with deft strokes of an astringent pad.

"I see, the universal Darling. Well, this is exactly how we are going to do it, Ms. Bocou." Edgar perched on a folding stool next to his number two camera, off to the side and slightly behind his uncle, so that he could observe without being observed. While he spoke, Gogo turned the attractive past-middle-aged woman into a ravishing young Hollywood siren.

"I'm going to take a set of 3-D pictures of you, super high-res, from every angle. Basically, I am going to map your entire face—"

"And throat."

"Yes, the throat too—"

"And I wonder about my bosom—" Bocou put a hand to the designer bib Gogo had draped over her dress.

"Your decolletage is still exquisite," Gogo assured her.

"Best to see how we do with face and throat first," Edgar hurried to add. This project was already interfering with his regular work, he did not need it to grow to the size of Bocou's breasts. "You see, I'm mapping every millimeter of your head and neck in order to generate a set of options for constructing the holographic image of your face around your face, in a way that changes with your movements and also with the angle from which you're viewed. It will be completely dynamic. If you blush, the image will blush, when you blink it will blink. An entire network of nanochips will continuously program itself based on kinetic, thermal and photovoltaic signals."

Bocou wanted to raise her eyebrows but didn't, with Gogo dabbing out the wrinkles on her forehead. "I confess, I didn't understand very much of that."

"Sorry. Why don't you ask me a question."

"Where do these nanochips go?"

"They are part of a sort of netting that you wear—"

"I'm going to have to wear a net over my head!?"

"Sweetheart, you have been wearing a veil for three months," Gogo chided her.

"I'm afraid there isn't any other way, short of appearing everywhere in a kind of projection box."

Bocou wanted to frown, but didn't, Gogo was starting on her lips.

"The nanochips are receivers, processors and emitters all in one," Edgar continued, warming to his subject. "Never been done before. Totally awesome. If you don't like it, I'll take it to the CIA. I mean, you could disguise a spy with this thing—"

"It's Bocou's, though, not the CIA's, Eddie," Gogo warned him. I think she'll like it." He sure hoped so, or he'd be fired by his exclusive client and have to beg the nerdnik for a handout. "There are just a couple of issues, though, sweetheart. Edgar, tell Bocou about the issues."

"Honestly, Uncle, I'm trying. I thought you had explained some of this already." Edgar and Gogo exchanged displeased looks, and Edgar continued, "What is going to happen, Ms. Bocou, is that the nanochips will project a set of tiny holographic tiles that will shift and change and overlap to create your digital face. No one will see it—the mask, let's call it—but if they were to touch it, well, it will be disconcerting, in that they will see their hand appear to go through your face and then will feel it touching this sort of net-like material."

"Oh my."

"I know. I told my uncle that it seemed awfully restrictive—not to be able to be touched."

"Oh, it's not that," Bocou whispered, trying not to move her mouth. "I never let anyone touch my face—they all know not to muss my makeup. But *I* will be *wearing* the thing. Won't I get shocked?"

"No, it won't use that much current. It'll run off a watch battery."

"Oh."

"Still, you'll need a special hairdo to hide the processor and plug-ins. We came up with two or three styles. Uncle Gogo will show you the sketches after we're done here."

"Well, you sound like you know what you're doing." Bocou wanted to cry at what she had gotten into, but Gogo was applying the last dusting of powder to set up his work.

"The kid's a genius. You just give him a chance to prove it," Gogo assured her. "Okay, Sweetie, open your eyes and look real pretty for the camera— Fabulous! Eddie, she's all yours."

□ □ □

After five more months of mysterious seclusion, Bocou came barreling back to first place on the celebrity charts.

She had two TV shows, a magazine, her own line of cosmetics, a clothing label and a Las Vegas act that was setting up for an international tour. Not bad for someone of such modest talent. She could sing in key, read passably from a teleprompter, walk and even dance a little on six-inch heels, and make an assortment of faces that looked a little like acting, assuming the emotion being depicted was gorgeous. Hardly anyone made the mistake of calling her Lillith anymore. It was like when Cassius Clay became Mohammed Ali. Folks were confused at first but quickly got over it, and they kept loving the iconic celebrity by her new name.

One of the reasons Bocou was so popular was that when she appeared in person she was like a vision—even more beautiful than on screen, and even more remote. A special sort of energy crackled around her and there were multiple witnesses to the "Bocou Aura"—literally a halo that emanated from her elaborate hairdos. Everyone wanted to see it with their own eyes. No one was put off by her unwillingness to be touched. Her manner was always so warm and beneficent. With the general paranoia about flus, drug-resistant bacteria, bedbugs, and even cholera in some of the countries where she traveled, Bocou was forgiven her extreme precautions to stay healthy. She was seen as a somewhat sad figure—infinitely lovable yet alone and unapproachable, a modern day Rapunzel.

Years went by and Bocou's beauty remained legendary. Despite her semi-tragic persona, she was mostly happy. Being adored from afar suited her. Being a legend in the flesh. She demanded that Edgar do more and more of her body—her bosom, then her hands and arms, eventually her feet and legs. She seemed to never age at all.

Late in life there were telltale signs of deterioration. Bocou's posture became odd, her hair wild. Her decline was attributed to the loss of her longtime makeup artist and companion of recent years, Gogo Forritt. Theirs had been a sort of Cinderella story in reverse—the beautiful and powerful princess had married the lowly—and older—swain. Unlikely as it seemed, their devotion had been genuine. Gogo joined Bocou in her seclusion, giving up his own social life to become exclusively hers. Bocou in turn doted on Gogo. She provided him with the best physicians, who kept the old man alive and functioning into his nineties.

Bocou, twelve years younger, did not last long after Gogo passed. She expired in their Chicago condo one February morning and was found by the landlord shortly after, when he entered the apartment seeking the source of a worrisome smoky smell. The burners were off and everything seemed to be in order, but his famous tenant was immobile and unresponsive under her satin covers. He called 911 from the threshold of her bedroom and looked no further for the source of the smell. If that was the smell of death, he did not want to get any closer.

The coroner unraveled Bocou's secret when he removed her wig, and he assured the police that she had not been the victim of some strange cult murder. Her face, hands, arms, legs and much of her torso were scarred in the pattern of a fine grid. In some places an actual webbing was melded to her skin. The once gorgeous Bocou looked like utter hell.

Chicago detectives contacted Edgar Forritt. He flew out from Palm Springs and told them the whole story, with his patent attorney by his side.

"She was supposed to take the damn things off every night!" Edgar swore under his breath, cursing himself and his uncle. What he had seen in the mortuary when he peeked under the sheet that covered Bocou's mangled flesh would haunt him for the rest of his days. "I can't believe he let her— All these years— I should have stayed near her after my uncle died. She needed me." Then he began to sob, thinking that, really, she hadn't needed him or his uncle at all. She was a natural beauty. Even her pores had been gorgeous.

The detective across the table drummed his fingers impatiently.

Edgar pulled himself together. "Well, if that's all, I need to tend to the funeral arrangements. I told the mortician I'd take care of everything."

Everyone who peered into Bocou's coffin remarked on how great she looked—at least what they could see. The glamour queen still required that the world keep its distance. Like a masterpiece in a museum, a velvet rope protected her from their breath. She looked utterly fabulous. The aura seemed to remain with her even in death.

When the viewing was over, the last guests noticed how Edgar Forritt, the heir who had stood at attention beside her all afternoon, closed the casket himself, and that the electricity flickered as he did so. The lights dimmed noticeably, multiple witnesses agreed, and when the casket lid clicked shut, it was like a singular light had gone out of the world never to shine again.

TSUNAMI

Alison gasps to wakefulness from her dreams of drowning, clasping the sheets in sweaty hands. She finds herself safely afloat her puffy mattress, sunlight splashing prettily across polished furniture. Everything is in its place—the rocker, the wardrobe, the long dresser holding a big satin-lined jewelry chest and a tray of expensive perfumes, the antique roll-top desk sporting a slim laptop. Alison inventories her elegant surroundings with, oddly, more regret than relief. She feels rumpled and out of sorts, and she notices that she's slept in her clothes—the same shorts and t-shirt she changed into yesterday after her errands . . .

. . . It all comes back to her: The horrific news of the earthquake and the tsunamis all around the Indian Ocean. Tens of thousands reported dead in a dozen countries. The full extent of the destruction yet unknown because so many areas are cut off from contact.

One tragic account after another had spilled out of the radio while she heated up leftovers from Antonio's and put together some salad. This was not the first time, by any means, that she'd shed some tears into her dinner while the reporters of National Public Radio brought tales of hardship and injustice to her well-equipped kitchen. Often she felt a twinge of guilt while listening to the news. There she was actually being *entertained* (what else could you call it?) by the misfortunes of others while she filled her belly with gourmet food at her marble countertop. Last night that twinge had become a stabbing pain. She'd needed two big glasses of red wine to get the food down, while the radio told her how, on the other side of the world, the sea had swallowed entire cities in one big gulp.

She could have turned on the TV to see the pictures coming in, instead she turned off the radio to sit in silence. Later she would go on-line and make a donation. For now she simply wanted to let herself feel, to grieve, as though those people were her own. She was more accustomed to holding the pain of others at bay. What was the point of hurting for people at a distance, people she didn't know and couldn't comfort? Those victims of civil wars and natural disasters were so far away, Alison had no sense of the lives they had lived, let alone what they had lost. She figured the best she could do was send a check and get on with her own life. But on this night her generosity felt meager despite the size of those checks. To have lost absolutely nothing and then to scrimp on mere tears was pathetic.

Alison poured a third glass and sat in the dark living room, unwilling to look at the designer-selected suite of furniture, the someday-valuable paintings collected in the course of many visits to Santa Fe . . .

She'd worked for every bit of it . . .

With a little help from Wall Street . . .

And the divorce settlement . . .

Well, she worked. Hard. And she liked nice things and was pleased to be able to support the arts, and the economy in general, by living nicely. She tried to imagine all of her beautiful things being washed out to sea or, a more likely threat to Alison in her Phoenix condo, swallowed up by the earth. At that point, if somehow she herself managed to survive, might she wish she hadn't? Imagine having lost everything, facing utter destitution. Imagine the dread of not knowing if help would come at all.

Death, Alison decided, in the absence of her friends, her work, and her possessions, would be a mercy. This was a little bit of comfort as she considered the demise of whole families, whole communities—at least they had gone together. She herself would not want to be the one who was spared, who had to keep battling for survival, grieving, suffering.

More realistically, Alison could easily have been one of the wealthy vacationers on the beaches of Thailand who had been washed out to sea—not a native surrounded by family. Now, in that case, she would be really bummed to be suddenly dead, to have abandoned her Phoenix palace for a foreign beach and left a beautiful mess behind. There was no little heir or heiress to get all her stuff, no husband (*his* gift would be the suspension of alimony payments). Her parents would get everything. But they'd have no idea of the value of anything, and in their grief they'd probably give it all away . . .

A horrible thought caused Alison to pour another glass of wine. What if they gave it all to Tommy anyway?! They wouldn't!

Alison tried to calm herself. She'd be dead, so why

should she care? At least it would put an end to her parents' deluded hope of a reconciliation.

Alison's wine-sodden mind was drifting from the Indian Ocean tragedy and returning to its natural state of self-absorption. She contemplated the question of which would be sadder: Alison without her possessions or the possessions without Alison. Eventually she stumbled to the bedroom, intending to type up an itemized list of bequeathals for her will, and collapsed on the bed to dream of vases and bicycles, cookware and clothing, skis and area rugs, all marching out of the house in a long line behind a small brown man playing a pipe, leading them out to sea.

And by morning she was drowning.

She is hung-over, and the stark December sunshine of Phoenix is not welcome, and neither is the Christmas-to-New Year's office holiday she had been eagerly awaiting. It would be a relief to go to work today, even with the headache—to distract herself with a cost analysis while drinking strong, fresh coffee that was delivered to her desk. Instead she is faced with a day of luxuries at the salon in preparation for a ski trip to Aspen. The thought of it is appalling. She will cancel. Everything.

Something happened in the night, in the dreams. The possessions left, up and hauled themselves away when no wave would take them. She followed and tried to make them come back, tried to drag them back, was almost dragged with them to the bottom of the sea. The sea spit her out into the morning and kept the rest. Everything that surrounds her now is illusion—it is all gone, it is all going.

Alison splashes water on her face, ignoring the soaps,

astringents and moisturizers. She grabs clean underpants and a tank top from the top dresser drawer without looking to see what color, then from the hook on the inside of her closet door she takes the khaki pants and long-sleeved white shirt she wears for her brief forays in the garden. Socks, sneakers. No decisions—she only has one pair of anything. In the kitchen she eats cereal dry from the box, looking out the window, wanting to be out of the house, away from all these things that don't exist anymore.

The sun is killer, but her head has stopped throbbing. She's walked all the alcohol out of her system. She has on her straw garden hat. The hat is good. She has a big to-go cup full of ice water. She's sipping through a straw. It's delicious. She never did make the phone calls. She has put all of her obligations out of her mind. Every step takes her farther away from them. The calendar is among the many burdensome possessions that have been swallowed by the wave.

Alison understands that the feeling of having nothing is restful to her only because she chose it. Again and again she tells herself, "The wave has wiped out everything," until she almost believes it. And it is too easy, too easy to shrug it all off, to say, "Take it, take all of it, it was weighing me down." She remains above the fray, still insulated from the suffering of her fellow humans.

And so she allows herself no kith or kin either. All who are dear to her must perish in the wave. She must be bereft. One by one she snuffs out the life of every co-worker, friend and relative. With each imagined loss she thinks, "Yet, I could go on. It would be hard, but I would make it."

This exercise engages Alison's attention for several hours and many blocks. Somewhere she disposes of the cup. No one interrupts her. No one walks in Phoenix. Instinctively, Alison follows shade and steers clear of on and off ramps to major roadways; she hardly notices where she walks. At first she is elated by her discovery that she would survive on her own. She knows who she is. She values herself. She has confidence. And stubbornness, strength.

But by the end of the fantasy she is wrecked. She has no true love. No one she could not live without. Who is she kidding? She doesn't have to imagine losing everyone she ever loved—she is bereft already, she has already had a true love and lost him.

At this, at last, Alison's feet falter. A great heaviness slows her step. Her body sags. She is back to wishing the tsunami had swept her under. Alison perceives that her fantasy of losing all is actually her real life—there already is nothing. She's a divorced woman with no more delusions about finding Mister Right. She thought she was doing okay without a mate. She had dates, activities, hobbies. Just yesterday her life had been embarrassingly full. But now she feels lacking, her life is lacking, and all those possessions and friends she's spent the last twenty hours systematically eradicating have always been lacking, but through no fault of their own. Alison blew it. She should have loved the objects less and the people more.

No doubt, much of Alison's feeling of emptiness stems from hunger, excess sun, relentless walking. She is aware of this, and recognizes that this is what the displaced feel also—the survivors—mental and physical anguish bound up together, so that when you most need your wits, your spirit wilts, your body is wasted. It is at this point that an outstretched hand means everything. Humans need each other more than anything.

Alison walks in a thin stripe of shade along the side of a community center. Now that she recognizes where she is, she can't believe how far she's walked. And she has nothing on her, absolutely nothing in her pants pockets but a gum wrapper and a used tissue. No wallet, no ID, no cash, no key! She wonders if she's locked herself out or left the condo open. Maybe everything really will have disappeared by the time she makes her way back. And the most miraculous thing is: She doesn't care. About how she will get back, or when she will get back, or what she will find, or who will be missing her. The last thing Alison had to jettison is finally gone. The guilt is gone. In the end, it was only ever Nature that called the shots—an earthquake, a broken heart, a touch of sunstroke . . .

"Here you go, girl. Don't crap out now, you're nearly there."

A weathered hand thrusts a paper cup under Alison's nose. She takes it gratefully. Iced tea from a mix, chilled, no ice. She drinks it all before looking at the man. He's grungy, skinny, and looks worried about her.

"Thank you so much. Did you say I was nearly—where?"

"The soup line. Come on around the corner."

Alison follows him. On the east side of the building, across a small plaza, a ragged group of people queue up for food. Alison falls into line and her rescuer leaves her without a word. She is shocked to find herself in a group of more than fifty people, when so recently she had felt she was the only one on the street. Even here she is alone—a few muted conversations rise from the line, but mostly everyone shuffles along quietly with an air of infinite patience.

They accept bowls of posole and warmed foil packets of tortillas from cheery volunteers. Big coolers of tea and juice are the last stop. Many walk away with their food to who-knows-where, leaving plenty of seats at nearby picnic tables for others to sit and eat. No one has spoken to Alison in line. She feels she is inconspicuous in her ratty garden clothes with the straw hat shading her face. When she reaches across the table to accept her portion she mutters "Thank you" but does not look up, and then she quickly moves along.

Paul's eyes follow Alison as he pushes another bowl into another pair of dirty hands. He observes that the woman in the straw hat did not have dirty hands. She had a manicure. And her shirt, while stained with grass, is still white—like a shirt that sees detergent now and then. The same goes for her trousers. And the straw hat is barely frayed. He watches the hat bob toward one of the more distant tables. The woman is stooped, limping a little, hurting, but not undernourished or sickly. She sits with her back to the gathering of givers and receivers. The young man giving out the posole keeps an eye peeled for any movement of the white shirt while he finishes his task.

Alison is feeling revived by the food and tea, it is a great relief to sit. She realizes that soon it will be time to think about a bathroom, and how on earth she will get home, but at this moment she is content. She cannot imagine a more satisfying conclusion to her day of walking and soul-searching than to be sitting exactly here, savoring thin but certainly homemade posole in a Styrofoam bowl and cool, sweet tea from a paper cup. She cannot remember a more delicious meal. She tips her bowl to her lips to get the last drop, and then quickly puts it down. Someone is sitting down across from her.

"Good posole," Alison says, not wanting to seem like she's running away, though that's what she's about to do.

"Mind telling me what you're up to?"

Startled, Alison looks into the face of a young man. A tag on his shirt reads: Paul, Volunteer, Phoenix Food Bank.

"Huh?"

"Reporter? TV? What's your angle? You're not starving."

"I was." Alison feels disoriented, but not embarrassed. She'd like to be left alone. The man—Paul—chuckles like she's said something funny.

"Okay, so you were hungry. What happened? You left your credit cards at home?"

She stares at him, hurt. Doesn't he understand?

"I've been through an earthquake," she says, "tidal wave."

Paul had left his apartment with everything on: the TV with the sound down, looping video of devastated coastline, ticker scrolling the death toll; the radio tuned to Newsband, broadcasting cellphone reports that were mostly static; and his computer, chiming out a tone every time a new e-mail message came in. Yes, he'd been following the news too, but he didn't feel like he was *in* it—not yet.

"That's on the other side of the world!" Paul tells Alison

sternly. He's had a little training in how to deal with psych cases. Rule One: Don't go along with their delusions.

Alison can hear that in his voice, that tone professionals use to get control of a situation. In Paul's face she sees an expression wavering between alarm and bemusement.

"Aftershocks," she tells him, meeting his eyes, "they can travel pretty far."

He tilts his head, caught off guard. "Yeah, I suppose so," he answers.

He's a good-looking kid. Alison feels old. She is aware now of how pathetic she must seem—a rich woman out slumming, feeling sorry for herself. She looks down at her empty bowl and says contritely, "I really did leave my wallet at home. I don't know what came over me. I just had to get out for a walk. I guess I've walked about fifteen miles."

"Hang out for a few more minutes. I'll give you a ride."

Alison mouths "Thank you," unable to look at him. Humiliated, her annihilation is complete now. Pride and dignity have been swept away with everything else. She waits compliantly, with infinite patience.

Paul resumes his duties. He completes every routine, trying not to rush too much, and keeps checking to make sure the white shirt doesn't bolt, or vanish. He hasn't even asked her name. He replays their conversation in his head. How strange of her to bring up the very thing that has been consuming his thoughts—out here on the soup line, away from the news reports, among people who are typically too stressed by their own misery to focus on distant horrors.

Paul works a little faster, thinking about how many new

messages will be waiting in his e-mail. It's wrong to be excited about a disaster, yet he is excited because he is going to help. He's already gotten on the list to go to Sri Lanka with the Red Cross. It's this thing he has about feeding people—he's a "good works" kind of guy. Otherwise the brutality of life is simply unbearable, and you have to be mindless in order not to feel it. Paul cannot be mindless. When he chose compassion, he chose action.

Boyfriends never see it that way. They don't like his scampering around to dangerous countries, coming back with weird intestinal bugs, and harping about tragedy in near and far places to the point that every pleasure is shadowed with guilt. He hasn't met one yet who wanted to go with. He has had affairs with other relief workers, but those guys have never come home with him. So he is on his own, per usual. No one begging him to stay. No one begging to come along. Maybe he likes it that way. So much less to lose.

Alison moves to the other side of the picnic table so that she can watch Paul work. She sees that he is watching her too. There is nothing romantic about the soup line. She looks like hell and is ten years his senior at least. But there is a mutual curiosity between them that verges on attraction, an attraction of the soul.

When Paul wipes his hands on a towel and starts walking toward her, Alison tells herself to get ready to go, not to delay him more than necessary. But her legs are unwilling to move now. She smiles wearily at Paul as she tries to stand.

"It's okay," he says, sliding onto the bench beside her. "I want to ask you something before we get going."

They are both mesmerized by the long, red-checked tablecloth one of the volunteers is shaking out in the breeze.

"Go ahead." Alison has no secrets, they have gone the way of everything else in her personal clearance sale. She feels like all emotion has been drained out of her as well. But with Paul's question, she finds that she can still be surprised.

"I'm going to Sri Lanka with a disaster relief group. I could get you on the team if you have a passport. You'd need to hurry up and get some shots. What do you think? Do you want to come along? Do you want to volunteer?"

"Yes. Absolutely. There's nothing I would rather do," Alison answers immediately. She turns to Paul, "How did you know?"

"It happens now and then," Paul says, standing up and helping Alison to her feet. "Someone shows up in the soup line, and it turns out they're on the wrong side of the table."

Alison squeezes his hand. "You are so right, Paul. You are so right."

BILL'S APHORISTIC APHRODITE

The speed dating session was not going well for Bill. He'd sat with five women already, each for five minutes, each less appealing than the one before. The club was packed and there were still plenty of women to meet, but he had a strong inclination to check out and not stay for the remainder of the hour. He looked down at the "dance card" that had been automatically generated when he signed in with his dating profile ID.

Eleanor Westerbrook. Discouraged as he was, he took an immediate dislike to her name. Too many syllables. Too old fashioned. Bill was not so self-unaware as to think any of that was her fault. He was reflecting his own feelings about his own name. Maybe that's why the computer put them together. Two lonely blue-bloods weighed down by syllables. *I wonder what her middle name is?* Bill thought, and he brightened now that he had a conversation starter.

His tablet told him to go to Table 10. Around him, other seekers of suitable companionship were dropping into their assigned seats with their assigned dates. Now he could see across the room to Table 10, where a decent-looking woman had settled and was scribbling in a small notebook. Feeling a twinge of excitement, he hurried over.

"Here I am!" he announced too loudly. The pretty redhead hastily tucked away her pad and pen. She looked up, smiled, and gestured to him to take a seat.

Bill liked that she hadn't leapt to her feet or stuck out her hand to be shaken. She had yet to speak, which was a little concerning. Maybe she was hiding something—a lisp or limp, a stain on her sleeve. Whatever. For this split second, as he settled into the chair across from her with what he hoped was a confident and unhurried air, he chose to assume that she was, in fact, as fine as her first impression.

"Sorry about not getting up." She broke the ice.

Definitely no speech impediment. Bill noted that her voice was nasal but not too high-pitched, with a mild New England accent. One more sentence, and he could probably place her home county if not the town itself.

"After running across this room every five minutes, well, uhm, I guess I'm pretty out of shape. You're not a fitness freak, are you?"

"Uh, no." Bill couldn't see a lot of her, but her shape looked pretty good to him. "You're not ten feet tall, are you?" he quipped back.

She laughed and extended a graceful hand across the table, "Nice to meet you. Call me El."

"Call me Bill." Bill was proud to offer a firm, dry handshake. His glands had not betrayed him, though he could feel his heat rising inside the foolish mandatory suit. Impulsively he added, "William Gregory Middleton The Third at your service." He brushed the top of her hand with his lips before releasing it.

She blushed, not shyly, and fake-fanned herself. "Eleanor Emily Jane Westerbrook. Of the Hartford Westerbrooks."

"—Hartford Westerbrooks." Bill said it along with her.

"Do you know my family?"

"I know accents."

"Really? I want to hear all about that."

"Let us walk together," Bill boldly suggested.

"Love to."

"I saw you writing with a pen and pad," Bill stated when they had escaped the club.

"A dying breed am I."

She was not ten feet tall, but she was tall—Bill's height or a smidge over. They walked shoulder to shoulder up Charles Street, turning their heads frequently to smile into each other's faces.

"You make me feel like I'm going back in time," Bill said. Around them, the brickwork of Beacon Hill harkened to past centuries.

"You make me feel like I've seen my future," El answered. Suddenly she stopped and produced her pen and pad. *You make me feel like I've seen my future*, she mouthed the words as she wrote them down, then she repeated them while counting syllables with the end of her pen. "You make me feel like I've seen my fu-ture."

Bill watched, intrigued, practically holding his breath.

"Ten," El muttered.

"Is that good?"

El looked up guiltily. "Sorry. I take my work everywhere. Can't ever let a good idea slip by. You never know when you'll get another."

"Another ten syllables?"

El smiled at the nice fellow she was about to fall in love with. "You didn't read my intro, did you?"

"Heck no."

They began walking again.

"Well, even ten syllables can be too many. I'm an aphorist, and sometimes an affirmationist. You know, greeting cards and bookmarks and stuff."

Bill raised his eyebrows.

"Right now I've got a gig writing the little sayings that go on the inside of candy wrappers."

Was she pulling his leg? Bill couldn't think of a thing to say, even in one of his funny accents.

"You really don't know what I'm talking about!"

El took Bill's hand and led him into DeLuca's Market. They went up and down all the aisles, getting distracted by the foods and each other, until El finally found what she wanted right there at the check-out.

"Of course. Point of purchase. Should've known." She grabbed half a dozen foil-wrapped chocolates out of a jar and paid seventy-five cents each for them.

Bill was completely smitten by the time he popped the first chocolate into his mouth. They were back out on Charles Street, loitering by a wrought iron gate.

"Now look inside the foil," El instructed before he could crumple up the two-inch square and toss it away. He brought the wrapper closer to see a few words in purple script on the silver interior of the pink foil.

"Life will surprise you," Bill read aloud. Then a second time, counting on his fingers, "Life will surprise you."

"Five!" El exclaimed. "One of my best ever. Just five syllables!"

Bill held the foil admiringly at arm's length and blew a kiss from his fingertips. "*Magnifique!* And you get paid for this?"

"*Mais oui!*" She tossed him another chocolate.

"Life will surprise you, alright."

"Oh, I've got a million of them," El bragged. And not one is longer than my name."

Bill watched El deftly unfold another pink foil and squint at the wrapping.

"Hah! That one! They insisted I write one with *Delicious* in it. I mean, c'mon, that's three syllables right off the bat. Dee-Lish-Us." She popped the candy into her mouth.

Bill didn't laugh. He had gone all googly eyes at her. She hastily finished the chocolate and dabbed at her lips with a tissue.

"My darling Eleanor." William Gregory Middleton The Third dropped to one knee right there on Charles Street and placed his hands over his heart. "Should you ever require a few more syllables, I beg you to share mine."

SILVER AND GOLD APPLES

The storefront on Easy Street had been standing vacant for almost a year when a young woman named Sun Flower picked up the lease. "That's Ms. Flower," she impressed upon the realtor, wanting to make clear that she had a first name and a last name, which were Sun and Flower respectively. Later, when they were signing the papers, she would graciously invite him to call her Sun. Ms. Sun Flower quickly went to work sweeping up her new place and installing half a dozen large paintings—not her own, "a friend's"—and a sign above the door that read: *Gallery of Dreams*.

She filled the long glass case by the front door with chewing gum, candy, cigarettes and condoms, upon the advice of the friendly realtor, who knew that this location originally housed a convenience store. He had personally seen a locksmith, a tailor shop, an accounting business and a religious bookstore come and go under this roof. The locksmith, the tailor and the accountant each lasted, and even prospered, by maintaining a small retail operation on the side to serve the needs of the immediate neighbors. One by one, they built a nest egg with which to relocate their ventures to higher class quarters.

"The only business that couldn't make it at 313 Easy Street," the realtor confided to Sun (he had asked her to call him Donald by then), "was The Good Book bookstore. Didn't sell a lot of books, and wouldn't carry tobacco or condoms, though they did have those chocolate covered peppermints."

Sun added *chocolate covered peppermints* to her list, and then *rolling papers*, but so Donald wouldn't see. Later she added *sunscreen*, *crossword & sudoku magazines*, and *pantyhose*. The long case became a marvel of useful provisions, enlivened by the occasional amethyst geode, beaded bracelet or antique pill box.

The neighbors were eager to support Sun's endeavor. She tried to keep a regular schedule, and if someone she knew rang the bell during off hours, she'd unlock and fill their order. She appeared not to care at all about making money, but rather acted as if she were there as a service, was unfortunately obligated to take money for the paltry goods she provided. Though Sun was happy for anyone to come in just to view the Gallery of Dreams, most people bought a little something. Some of the locals came in frequently, hoping to learn what Sun was really up to. It was not at all apparent, but they liked Sun, and they liked the paintings, which seemed to change often although no one ever noticed large paintings being moved in and out of the store. A regular clientele developed, half curious and half enchanted.

The women were more often the curious ones, and the men more often enchanted. Donald was both, and he came to the gallery more than anyone, and stayed longer, under the pretext of taking a business interest in Sun's success. Sun liked Donald a lot, and she was torn between the desire to take him into her confidence and the fear that if she did he would disappoint her. She enjoyed his company, and so she said nothing that would put him off her, or her off him—that is, she did not put their friendship to the test but kept things very flirty and coy.

One day Donald was sitting in the store on the recently installed vintage naugahyde bench enjoying the new paintings (which Sun insisted were the same six she had started with) when a woman came in, took a long time at the counter buying her chewing gum, and finally, with a backward glance at Donald, confided to Sun that she had had a very unusual dream that morning. This appeared to interest Sun tremendously and she leaned close over the counter and consulted with the woman for long minutes. Donald pretended to be absorbed in the paintings, which formerly he was, but now he wasn't, and he leaned forward with his elbows on his knees and one hand lightly cupping his ear, but he still couldn't make out their words. Then Sun called over to him to please mind the counter for a few minutes. She led her customer to the back of the store and through a door that led to the storage area, back exit, and the stairway up to her apartment.

Donald wondered how Sun would respond to *his* dreams, especially the one about being admitted through that very door and up those stairs! Dutifully, he went behind the glass counter, pulled out his phone, and was soon absorbed in catching up on his real estate business.

The next thing he knew, Sun was spritzing glass cleaner on the counter top and giving it a good cleaning, making much of squeezing around Donald as he perched on the single stool in the narrow workspace. Her behind wiggled as she wiped the glass, and he put his hand on it. She turned around and they lurched into each other's arms, but almost immediately the door chime sounded and they jumped apart.

The chime— "What happened to the lady with the dream?" Donald asked softly, sliding around to the public side of the counter. "I never heard her go out."

"I let her out the back," Sun answered even more quietly, then she turned a radiant smile toward the new customer and spoke loudly.

"Hi there! Can I help you?"

The disheveled old man—or was it a woman? it was hard to tell from the back—was already lost in the Gallery of Dreams. He/she stood staring.

"Go ahead and sit for a while, if you like," Sun practically shouted.

No response. The person was obviously hard of hearing. Sun and Donald smiled at each other, considering their interrupted embrace. For the sake of propriety, their relationship would now have to move beyond the confines of the store.

"I have to run, but can I see you tonight? Take you to dinner?" Not exactly the way he'd practiced, but it would do. Donald was clasping Sun's hand across the counter.

"Sure, that would be nice. Any time after six."

"I will be here one minute after six." Not likely, given traffic that time of day, but it sounded good. They squeezed hands before releasing each other to their respective duties, Donald to show an apartment on the east side of town and Sun to inquire as to the needs of the crumpled old—

Man. It was definitely a man. He turned around as soon as the door had chimed open then clicked closed with Donald's exit.

"Sorry to intrude," he rasped, gesturing to the door. "Seems like a nice fella."

"And what can I do for you, sir?" Sun didn't like the feeling that he'd been spying on her. In her line of work she had seen every possible kind of scam and scam artist. Going around as a deaf or blind beggar was a classic. Sometimes, scam or no, she'd go along with it. Scamming and begging are hard work—a person who can make it that way, given half a chance, might have the fortitude to make it some other way. And that was Sun's business, after all, the distribution of half-chances.

"Sir?" The old man's attention had drifted back to the paintings. "Excuse me, sir, did you come in for something in particular?"

He shook himself as if struggling out of a dream, then slowly retrieved the idea that had brought him there. "Yes, ma'am. I came in for an apple. Do you have an apple?"

Sun gave the man a piercing look, but his eyes met hers and held steady. "Silver or gold?" she finally asked.

"Silver, ma'am. Just silver. Just a little something for food and shelter."

Sun nodded and stepped around the counter. She turned the latch in the door to the street, and the sign in the window from *Open* to *Be Back Soon*. "Come with me . . ."

". . . And I led him back to the courtyard, to the two trees my parents gave me, and I let him pick one apple from the silver apple tree and sent him on his way."

"A single silver apple?" Donald tried to sound amused and not angry. What kind of joke was this, after they'd had such a great evening together?

They were sitting on the cushioned bench in the locked and darkened store, holding hands. Before Sun could answer, a movement from the direction of the paintings caught Donald's eye. The middle painting was reconfiguring itself from a sort of syrupy tiger stalking through a jungle into a field of wiggly wheat bordered by an orchard.

"Uh, did you just see that painting change?"

"It's only the shadows, and the lights from the cars passing by," Sun answered too quickly, and she jumped up to turn on a bank of lights.

"Ouch!" Donald squeezed his eyes shut and then opened them again slowly. The painting in question showed a wheat field bordered by apple trees. "But I'm sure that middle one had been a tiger in a jungle."

"Really? Interesting. The paintings are like clouds, Don, people see different things in them."

It was the first time she had called him Don. He looked toward her to read her expression, but she flicked the light off quickly.

"What's going on here, Sun?"

"I just want to explain about the apples first."

"All right, then you'd better show me." He stood.

Sun came over and took his hand, which was clammy now—not deliciously warm as it had been all evening each time he touched her, which had been often. She led him to the back of the store, hoping that she was doing the right thing. Donald had to know the truth if they were going to keep going. She had to either do this or dump him, and it was too late to dump him. She was already in love.

Donald's life—his life after Sun came into it—was flashing before his eyes, from the very first day when he had shown her the property and she had been ecstatic about the sad little patch of dirt behind the store, right up to their recent romantic dinner in which Sun had casually referred to her parents as "keepers of trees" and he had envisioned nothing more unusual than a pair of hippy arborists. In between, there had been many companionable hours with Sun in the store, and almost as much time spent listening to the gossip about her over at the Oasis Lounge. And through all of that, despite all of the unusual and mysterious components of her business, he had never entertained the notion that anything unnatural was at play. Now, he stepped through the door he had dreamed of stepping through, and asked quite seriously, "Is this a dream? Has everything been a dream?"

"No," Sun answered sharply. "This may not conform to your notion of reality, but it's not a dream."

They traversed the dingy hallway, passing the purple-curtained stairway of Donald's desire, and stood at the back door with its bright red EXIT sign. Donald figured he had nothing to lose. Their first date had already veered far off course, and whatever lay beyond that door was likely to derail the whole evening. He took Sun in his arms and kissed her until her knees began to buckle.

"That, Ms. Sun Flower, is my notion of reality."

Sun almost made a u-turn to lead him upstairs, but she regained her resolve. "You need to see this."

She snapped back the deadbolts and ushered Donald through to the courtyard, where two apple trees grew—

impossibly and uncomfortably—to about seven feet. The earth was hard-packed and barren right up to their trunks; no effort had been made to cultivate, weed or water any part of the small yard. The brick walls had been built up a bit, sloppily, just enough to shield the trees from the neighbors' view. The unwatered trees were sparsely leafed so that the fruit was clearly visible—perfectly formed and polished silver apples on one tree, and gold ones on the other. It was a strangely ugly sight, for being trees and treasure. Donald stepped close, carefully examined the leaves and bark and apples, and stepped away again.

"I really don't know where to begin, Sun. Do I have to ask a million questions or will you just tell me what this is?"

"These are the trees that my parents tend. There are different kinds for different places, depending on the custom, the myths, what is considered precious. They are simply a way to give charity. That is my job."

"The simple way would be to hand out money. This is—way over the top!"

Sun smiled. "No, it is not a simple way, I agree. But you know what I mean, Don. There is no other purpose to this than to offer help."

There it was again, *Don*—not endearing, but insincere, cajoling—*let's not go there*.

"Are you sure? No other purpose? Who are your parents, anyway? How is this even possible? What the hell is this?" Donald felt fear rising up from his gut—the way it had when he'd confronted something incomprehensible over there, in that incomprehensible war—and he was shooting off his mouth like a weapon. But when he saw Sun's stricken expression, a wave of love and protectiveness brought him to his senses. “I mean, what do you tell the IRS?”

That broke the tension. They each took a deep breath.

Sun went over to the silver apple tree and said, “Here, take one apple, and I will tell you exactly what I told the old man this morning, and then you can see for yourself what it’s all about.”

“Why not a gold apple?”

“You are not in need, I shouldn’t give you any.”

“Did the woman this morning get a gold apple?”

“Yes. When there are children involved, I always give the gold apple, even if they don’t ask for it.”

“Oh.” Donald noticed that Sun was different in her capacity as giver of precious apples. Sort of saintly. Or a Greek goddess in the flesh.

“Go ahead and take your apple now.”

“I have to pick it myself?” Sun nodded. He could not help feeling that he was being tested. Defiantly he stepped close, took hold of the nearest apple and plucked it from the tree, resisting the childish urge to look for the biggest and best one. “Now what?”

“In the morning, take it to that little place on Pantry Lane. You know, the one with a shoe repair on one side and appliances on the other?”

“Mr. and Mrs. Carson? You’re kidding.”

“I thought you would know them.”

“They were practically my first clients. Had the appliance business, and took over the shoe repair from old Mr. Farrell. Mr. Farrell *was* my first client.”

“I just thought you would know them because you know everybody. I didn’t know they were special.” Sun tilted her head as if this was meaningful.

"So, they'll know what to do with this?" Donald looked down at the cold, hard thing that did not warm in his hand, then hastily put the silver apple in his pocket. Regardless of how much or little he could get for that oddity, he was already anxious to be rid of it. Before a new feeling of dread could wash over him, he reached for Sun.

"The mystery of it all will drive me crazy. I wonder what we can do for distraction until morning."

Sun took Donald upstairs.

Mrs. Carson would not touch the silver apple Donald placed in front of her on the counter. The surprise she registered at seeing it had to do with Donald and not the apple. She peered at him through thick glasses with a combination of concern and disappointment.

"Have you fallen on hard times, Donald?"

"No. Things are pretty good."

"Then what are you doing with this?"

Donald wished she would pick it up and stash it somewhere before another customer came in. "It was, uh, given to me so I could learn, uhm, learn what it does." he stammered.

"Given to you? Who gave it to you?"

He could tell she thought he'd stolen it. She still refused to touch it.

"Sun," he whispered, "Sun Flower. She let me pick it from the tree and told me to bring it to you. She, we, well, she thought it was something I should know about."

"Well, that's a new one." Mrs. Carson pursed her lips and stared at the apple. She did not let on that it was news to her that the apples came from an actual tree or were distributed by Sun Flower. Though, now that she thought about it, that last part made sense. Not a surprise was that Donald loved Ms. Sun Flower. Everyone knew that.

"All right. Tell me what you need." She put the apple in a paper bag and set it down again on the counter between them.

"I need to know how this works," Donald said without hesitation.

"Hmmph. I don't know how *this* works. Normally, I would take the apple and ask you what you need. You might say shoes or food or a roof over your head or a new suit. On my part, it might be as simple as opening the cash register and giving you fifty bucks, or a couple of hundred. Or I could send you on to someone else."

"And where do *you* trade in the apples?"

Mrs. Carson nodded to the bag and said, "Take it to my husband and tell him you want to go along with him. He's back in the office getting ready to go to the bank."

Donald did as he was told, feeling like he was finally getting somewhere. He was more than happy to allow that nothing untoward or unnatural was going on. Mr. Carson would take the apple to the bank with his deposit from the shop, and a philanthropic transfer would take place behind the scenes. The trees and apples were simply props in some eccentric's charitable scheme, with Sun, her parents and the Carsons acting as the agents. It was probably even legal.

Mr. Carson left Donald holding the bag, literally, double-parked and motor running, while he dashed in with his deposit. Donald stared at the bank entrance impatiently between nervous glances left and right and in the rearview mirrors. His hope for a reasonable explanation for the silver and gold apples evaporated. It was replaced by the unpleasant sensation of being a player in a game not of his devising:

He was on a quest for secret knowledge. He had been drawn into the game by a fair lady to whom he must now prove himself. She had given him a magic apple and two guides, Mr. and Mrs. Carson. Missing, so far, was an opponent. But there would certainly be one—an actual opponent or a set of obstacles would materialize as soon as Donald began getting close to discovering the secret. That's how these things worked. He watched everyone on the street carefully, expecting someone to approach the car and demand the apple; or maybe a cop or meter reader would pull up to harass him. Opponents. Obstacles. Donald felt his prickly soldier senses kick in. While he messed around with the side mirror to better see anyone coming from behind, Mr. Carson emerged from the bank and hurried back to the car. When the driver's door opened, Donald jumped.

"Someone didn't get enough sleep last night," Chuck Carson observed while Donald rubbed his head. "Could you put that damn thing on the floor—it looks like you're drinking."

Donald put the paper bag on the floor and surrounded it with his feet so it couldn't get away. "What now?" he asked, as if there might actually be an answer.

"Damned if I know. Never had company along before." Mr. Carson turned on the car's navigation system and a female voice asked, "Where to?"

"Apples," Carson suggested, rolling his eyes at Donald. Before Donald could laugh along, a map appeared on the dashboard display and the voice was instructing Mr. Carson to proceed north to Posey Blvd. and east to the freeway... The men looked at each other. "This some kind of joke?" Mr. Carson grumbled uneasily.

"No way! You think *I'm* joking? What would you normally do with the apple?" Donald demanded irritably. He for sure had not had enough sleep.

"I'd drive around a little until I saw a guy with apples—"

"Any guy with apples or the same guy every time?" Donald had *never* seen an apple vendor downtown.

Mr. Carson pulled out into traffic and proceeded north as instructed by the voice. "I guess there's two or three different ones. I never had trouble finding them. Seemed like they always popped right out from nowhere a block or two from the bank there, and I'd say, 'I'll give *you* an apple if you give me an apple.'"

"Who told you to say that? Who gave you the instructions the first time?"

"The same guy who told me to never bring anyone along, that's who!"

Donald told himself not to blow it. He asked more gently, "So, you give the guy a silver apple and he gives you a real one?"

"Something like that." Carson was clamming up.

"And all you get for helping people is a fresh apple?" Donald asked lightly, like it made no difference to him.

"And then something shows up in my bank account, and it's always enough," Carson said, clearly not inclined to divulge numbers.

"I just don't get it," Donald complained. They were close to the freeway entry now.

"Me neither. Honest. And I'm gonna have to stop for gas if this route here is for real."

Donald gaped at the display. Their destination was in the next county, Flower's Tree Farm.

Sun could not face the day. At first she lay in bed luxuriating in the soft sheets that smelled of love-making. But soon she was overcome with worry. She longed for Donald, but he'd gone off to chase down her secrets. If he learned them, he might bail out—and if he didn't, she wouldn't want him. She needed someone who wasn't afraid of the truth, a lesser man would not last long with her.

Sun heard someone ringing the bell and then knocking on the store window below. She slid out of bed and put on her robe to go peek between the blinds. All she could see was the top of a woman's head. It was probably Mrs. Lands expecting to be let in for a box of cough drops. Sun refused to go down. She pulled away from the window just as the woman looked upward.

Sun made sure her door was bolted, then took a long shower. Donald would not be back for a while— She refused to think, *If at all.* So much hung in the balance, but their love was not to be questioned. It had built slowly over months through Donald's shy wooing and Sun's subtle encouragement. They had come to know each other well despite the secrets she kept from him and the odd things he refused to ask her about, until last night.

Sun was angry at herself for not answering him in more detail. She had intended to tell him everything, but when the time came, she couldn't summon the energy. That had been the moment to defy her parents for the man she loved, but instead she was subjecting him to their whims. Why couldn't she decide for herself if he was trustworthy?

But she had. He was. Honest, courageous and true. And persistent. Donald would ferret out all that she could have told him, as well as the answers she herself had never learned.

Donald and Mr. Carson did not speak on the forty-mile ride to Flower's Tree Farm. Carson pulled over once to call Mrs. Carson and tell her they were on "kind of a long ride." Donald, leaning far to his left ostensibly to adjust his wallet in his back pocket, strained to hear what she said in reply. Something about being careful, and a washing machine part she had left in the trunk, and what would he do for lunch. Wifely things.

While Carson drove in surly silence, Donald found himself mentally reviewing a parade of lovely women he had chosen not to court. Why, he wondered, could he not have settled down with one of them? There were three or four who would certainly have accepted him, a couple were downright heartbroken that he didn't propose. He was a smart, pleasant-looking man, tested in combat, successful in business. Women liked him, and sometimes he saw in their eyes happy calculations about children and future comforts. A little of that was flattering, but too obvious and he would split. Why? he wondered, why? He wanted a companion, he wanted a family. He wanted nothing more than a comfortable normal life in the little community where he'd settled after his army discharge and where he knew every lane and alley and every building inside out.

But, if Donald *had* hitched up with someone by now—by

then, when Ms. Sun Flower had entered his life—would that really have made him safe? Or would he have fallen head over heels even so? After last night, it was impossible for Donald to imagine resisting Sun under any circumstances. When they had stepped into her apartment and fallen into each other's arms, it was with the confidence that their love was meant to be.

That they both felt this way, that the feeling which had been creeping over them all through dinner remained even after the awkwardness of the apple trees, magnified the sense of rightness, of destiny. The friendship they had patiently tended for months was bursting forth into full-blown love. Yet, after all those months, Donald knew absolutely nothing about his beloved. Less than nothing, because none of the things you could usually take for granted about a person, any person, seemed to apply. Sun had parents who grew precious metals on trees, she had magic paintings hanging on her walls, she kept secrets she didn't know the answers to herself.

By the time Mr. Carson pulled down a lane shaded by perfectly normal sycamore trees, Donald was damp with anxiety. He was about to meet Sun's parents. He loved Sun and wanted to marry her and needed to know everything about the trees and the apples and what she did, what they all did for a living. He was clear about the questions he must ask. But what did he really expect, or want, for answers?

After she had failed to receive one customer, Sun expected that they would all show up, pressing their nosy noses to the storefront glass and lobbing nickels at the upstairs window to try to rouse her. But, to her relief, the street had become quiet—more like they were all staying away on purpose. She dressed and descended to the store, but she did not turn the sign or the lock. She put on one bank of lights and sat with her chin in her hands, staring at the paintings in her Gallery of Dreams.

Sun wondered, not for the first time, if all children of experimental psychologists endured what she did. Though "endured" would be putting it too strongly. The Flowers were well-meaning, they loved their daughter, and Sun was originally drawn into their research as if it were a game. She found it fun, never manipulative or abusive. At least not at the time. And if it hadn't felt that way then, and if no harm was done—then no harm was done, right?

Sun wondered. Her parents were at the top of their field, or had been once. How skillfully had they brainwashed her that she, to this day, could not say what thoughts and actions were truly her own? Still, wasn't all child-rearing like that? Training, modeling, molding—call it brainwashing if you want to be dramatic. That's what the good doctors would say. "Conditioning from an early age is what raising children is all about."

Sun wondered why her parents' research had to be kept secret for so long. How many years had it been since they applied for a patent on the "paintings"? They maintained they had never received it, it was still pending and had to be kept quiet. But the fundamental liquid crystal technology was ubiquitous by now, so what was the big deal?

The way her father explained it, each painting was composed of ultra-thin LC layers that responded to heat and light with such sensitivity that the warmth of a human body several feet away could cause a shift in the "visible canvas."

Sun had never seen them change that quickly, but Donald had—just last night. And then there was that guy who had once complimented her on the "projection devices"—*he* must have noticed something. But usually it was a subtle process, and those who saw—or caused—the paintings to change would rub their eyes but say nothing. Probably that was the very nature of the experiment, as with the apples, to see how people would behave when confronted with the unexpected. And so the truth behind the illusion *always* had to be kept secret . . . ?

Sun wondered why she had none of that curiosity about people that her parents had. She enjoyed the paintings and watching people look at them. She herself hardly noticed when they changed, and she didn't try to. She didn't see why she should bother. Radio frequency chips—another "patent pending" secret—embedded in the paintings' layers relayed information back to her parents. Same for the apples, so there was very little required of Sun except to provide the setting in which these marvels might be shared and reactions to them measured.

A rap on the door made Sun jump up guiltily. She was supposed to be open for business and sharing. She flipped on the rest of the lights and went to the door. It was Mrs. Carson.

"Are you okay, honey? Mrs. Lands came by and said she couldn't rouse you."

"No, she couldn't. I slept in, took a long shower."

"Well, good for you. A girl needs some 'me' time sometimes."

Sun was glad to have Mrs. Carson's company. She wasn't an especially warm woman, but she had a reassuring air of unflappability. "You think I should open up now?" Sun asked, expecting that her visitor might want a private chat.

But Mrs. Carson said, "Why not? The place is all spruced up, and I see the paintings have been rotated."

"Uh, yeah. Donald helped me with that last night." Sun turned the sign in the door and left it unlocked. She walked slowly behind the counter, feeling confused.

Mrs. Carson came over and leaned her elbows on the glass, covering the PLEASE DO NOT LEAN ON GLASS sign. "Donald came by this morning with a silver apple, and he mentioned you, which was a surprise, but then it wasn't," she said matter-of-factly. "He's a terrific fellow, one of our most eligible bachelors—but not anymore, I guess."

Sun blushed, and to her dismay the entire row of paintings behind Mrs. Carson reddened perceptibly.

"Well, I think that's just fine. And I don't care to know anything more than I do already about the apples. It's a peculiar process, but it's a help to people. And I trust Donald. You're right to trust him, too. If there's anything shady about it, he'll know what to do— Why are you laughing?"

"Shady—apples—get it?"

Mrs. Carson shook her head in exasperation. "Honestly."

"I'm sorry. But I assure you, there's nothing shady about the apples or even the trees they come from."

Mrs. Carson furrowed her brow and forbade herself to ask to see the apple trees, though she desperately wanted to. Her husband was already drawn in too deeply, she needed to relay her message and get back to her own shop.

"The thing is, after I sent Donald off with Chuck to do

whatever they do with the apples, a young man came in and asked *me* for an apple. That had never happened before, and I was suspicious and a little frightened."

"Oh my, of course." Mrs. Carson had Sun's full attention now.

"'Are you hungry?' I asked. 'Don't you want more than an apple?' I had some snacks in the office, but I was afraid to go back there with him or to leave him alone in the store. He said not to bother, and then gave me a box and told me to give it to the 'Golden Apple Lady,' and then he left real quick because Paul and Jack were out front unloading a busted gas stove." Mrs. Carson brought a square brown gift box out of the big sleeve of her coat and placed it on the counter. The two women looked at it quizzically. Sun supposed there would be a gold or silver apple inside—the box was just about the right size.

"It's not heavy enough to be an apple, any kind of apple," Mrs. Carson said. Then, when Sun didn't pick it up, "I'll let you open it in private." There was disappointment in her voice.

"No no, please stay." Sun lifted the box, feeling its lightness, and peeled back a bit of tape. She opened the lid a little, then all the way. "Well, I'm not sure—" She tipped the contents onto the counter.

The object also seemed to be made of brownish cardboard, marked with unusual symbols and what looked like mathematical formulas, which had been folded into a triangular tube then twisted and creased in five places to bring the ends together and create a bulky circlet.

"What do you think? A bracelet?" Mrs. Carson picked it up and slid it over Sun's left hand. "Oh, I'm sorry. There I go again. I shouldn't have touched it without asking."

Sun stared at the object on her arm. Her brain was itching like she was supposed to remember something. "No. It's okay. I think you're right. There was no other message? Are you sure?" Sun dug around in the box, then fingered the strange object on her arm. The symbols were ever so slightly raised. "I guess the message is right here, if I could decipher it."

June and Julius Flower were both tall and straight like trees, olive-skinned and of indeterminate ethnicity. Donald was tempted to guess African, but they were too fair for that. Both had grey hair. Sun was a brunette. At first Donald had thought her a tall Polynesian. Sun herself would only say that the family was from Scandinavia originally, and she'd never known her grandparents. In fact, she had barely known her parents. They kept her in boarding school. They disappeared for a while and were thought dead—she was vague about it. Donald suspected she had blocked out much of her unhappy childhood, and he took an immediate dislike to the parents. But now, here he was, meeting them in person—with Mr. Carson as a witness.

Assuming Mr. Carson remembered any of it. The Flowers seemed to have the older man under a spell almost from the minute they seated their guests and served tea. Before Donald could utter a word, Carson asked the first of a series of questions to which the Flowers took turns giving rehearsed-sounding answers—a whole lot of b.s. to Donald's ears. But Carson nodded emphatically throughout each monologue, and then jumped in with another question at the end as if on cue. The effect was hypnotic, and Donald pretended to zone out—since that's obviously what the Flowers wished—while trying hard not to.

Mr. Carson asked, "Why apples? Why not just give away cash?" Mrs. Flower responded at length about the psychological barrier to accepting charity versus a windfall, a charm, an inexplicable event. Plus, the gift of a silver or gold apple was so unusual, so implausible, that the donations were usually kept secret. That meant Sun never had a rush of people coming around, or the dreadful media.

Mr. Carson asked, "Is there a big organization keeping track of the apples?"

"A little organization," Mr. Flower admitted. "And the apples contain a homing device. We get them back as quick as we can and then send them out again . . ."

While their host elaborated, Donald decided it was unlikely that Sun was putting recycled silver and gold apples back on the trees. He'd seen the trees. The bark was realistic-looking, even up close, but was not natural—some high-tech material wrapped around a tree-shaped structure with artfully crafted silk leaves. The stems of the apples were thin tubes poking out of the trees' "limbs," from which the apples appeared literally to "grow." When Donald had picked an apple, the stem did not come with it, and a small silver bead immediately began to form at the end of the tubule.

"Why us?" Mr. Carson asked.

Mrs. Flower actually offered a simple, sincere answer, "Because you and your wife are worthy, Mr. Carson." Then she eyed Donald critically.

Donald gazed back with a fake blank stare and asked in the same serious tone Carson had used: "What about the paintings?"

The Flowers exchanged a look, and then Mrs. Flower began to speak in a very soothing voice that Donald found hard to resist. Each time she said the words "liquid crystal" he could feel his eyelids drooping lower. He forced himself to speak, aware that Carson was nodding heavily over his teacup.

"Do the feelings of the person who's looking cause the painting to change, or does the painting change the feelings of the person who's looking?"

Sun's parents glared at Donald. He stared back passively.

"Well, you see it's like this, Don," Mr. Flower began, and after that "Don"—the same way Sun had said it when she sounded so not like herself—Donald was not about to let down his guard. He renewed his effort to remain alert and skeptical through the Flowers' explanations about the apples and the paintings, their "research," and their daughter's task.

Straining to hear and remember every word, to look entranced but stay alert, Donald soon had a ringing in his ears. It was intermittent. It almost shadowed the pauses and inflections of Mr. and Mrs. Flower's speech. Donald focused more of his attention on the whine. It became a recognizable language, as if he had tuned in to a distant radio station. Maintaining a bland expression, he directed his attention to the second voice, the subliminal voice. Was it no more than his own imagination, overstimulated from stress, lack of sleep and the strangeness of the past twenty-four hours? Or was it—the voice of Truth?

Donald asked, "How are the apples made?"

The Flowers seemed glad that Donald had heard enough

about the paintings. They returned eagerly to the subject of apples. Mr. Flower began to talk about metallurgy and molds, while the faint, second voice in Donald's head said: *"The apples consist mainly of pollutants drawn from the environment and trapped in a metallic material that renders them inert."*

"What happens to the apples?"

"They are redistributed. If they become damaged they are melted down and remolded," Mr. Flower was happy to explain.

Donald also heard him say—it did sound like Mr. Flower, whispering: *"They will be recycled into fuel. In time they will be used for transport."*

"Transport to where?" The words were out before Donald could stop himself. The Flowers looked at him aghast, and then at each other. "I mean, where are they stored? How are they moved around? Do you hire a Brinks truck?" Donald tried to recover.

"That's a very good question, Don." Mrs. Flower began a long explanation of the storage facilities on their farm and the general "cover" of being farmers when they were really experimental psychologists with a big, secret endowment.

The relief Donald felt at avoiding a direct confrontation with Sun's parents was his undoing. The little voice spoke no more.

Donald woke with a start when Mr. Carson clapped him on the shoulder and said, "Let's go, kid."

"Where are the Flowers?" Donald whispered.

"Getting us something, they said. Let's get going before we have to accept any gifts. They've been plenty nice enough."

"Yeah, plenty nice."

The Flowers came in with a basket of apples, real apples, and some jam and things for Mr. and Mrs. Carson. They gave a smaller basket to Donald, along with a little paper box.

"Open it when you're with Sun," Mrs. Flower said, and patted his hand.

The men mumbled some thanks, stashed their baskets in the trunk, and drove back to the city in silence.

Donald's car had a couple of tickets on it by the time he got back to the appliance shop. He grabbed them, harrumphed, and jumped in the car without retrieving his fruit from Mr. Carson's trunk. He had the little box in his jacket pocket. He went to his apartment and paced around, took a shower, listened to his messages. Returned some calls. Nothing from Sun. He hadn't expected it. He would have to go see her. He had to look again at the apple trees, the paintings, her.

He stopped at the Oasis. He needed a drink before he could go see her. The place was abuzz with gossip about Sun and how she hadn't opened the store until Mrs. Carson went by to check on her, but apparently everything was okay—Sun just needed a morning off.

"She was probably tired from changing out all the paintings," Mrs. Lands opined, like one in the know.

"Again?!"

They were all off and running on another round of speculation about Sun and the Gallery of Dreams. Then they noticed Donald—one by one, nudge by nudge—until everyone had shut up or was talking about the weather.

Donald tossed down his martini, gave a nod to no one in particular and tried for a casual exit.

There was another ticket under his wiper, which was so not a surprise that he just stuck it in his pocket with the others, popped a breath mint, and drove determinedly to Easy Street. The gin was doing its job. He pulled up to the curb in front of the shop, possibly a hair too close to the hydrant, nosing over into yellow paint territory. He was tempting fate now. Daring the divine forces to strike again. He approached the darkened store. Before he could ring the bell, Sun opened the door for him.

The first thing he noticed was how much she looked like them. Her coloring, her willowy figure. There was no doubt about their kinship. Which made things more complicated. She pulled him inside and closed the door quickly. He pulled her to him. Their embrace was reassuring but brief.

"Did you meet them?" Sun asked, studying Donald as he stared at the paintings. He noticed that they had all taken on a reddish cast.

"Your parents. Yes."

"What did they tell you?"

"About what you do. The charity. And their work, a little bit. And they told me about the paintings, too."

"Really?"

"I'm not sure I believe them."

"It's hard to know what to believe with my parents."

Donald didn't doubt that she was as much in the dark as he. "Yeah, major mindfuck," he muttered under his breath, and then, "They gave me something." He took the box out of his pocket. "They said to open it with you."

Sun knew what was inside. But what did it mean? That he

had passed inspection? She was at a loss for words.

"Let's go upstairs," Donald suggested. The paintings were creeping him out. And Sun's expression told him he might want to be sitting down when he opened the box . . .

But it was just a weird construction of recycled cardboard, summer-camp-craft quality, with symbols and an interesting shape. When Sun stuck out her arm and showed him one just like it on her wrist, they couldn't help laughing.

They put the bracelets aside and made love. It was as good as last night. They said, "I love you," to each other and it felt and sounded right. Finally, Donald was able to ask the question he had been rehearsing for many hours.

"Sun, are your parents, uuhhmmm, uh, human?"

"They're as human as I am," she giggled. Donald had just had ample opportunity to discover any unhuman parts.

"Yeah, right, I mean, you sure seem human, and they do too, but—"

Sun rolled onto her side. He was only digging himself in deeper. He rolled over too and fit himself around her. "I love you," he told her again. "I don't care how freaky your parents are—I mean, seem. I'm the one with the problem, obviously."

Sun pretended to sleep. Her parents were freaky. Maybe they were space aliens. But she felt safe in Donald's arms. He had seen the apple trees. Had noticed the paintings, had met her parents—and he had come back. They would face the mysteries together. Whatever the truth turned out to be, Donald would give her the strength to accept it.

"I love you, Donald."

"I knew you weren't asleep."

Sun woke in the night and felt that Donald was no longer beside her. She quickly pulled on a sweatshirt and jeans and slipped into her moccasins. Light from the streetlamp outside sliced onto the dresser through cockeyed Venetian blinds. Her keys were gone. So was Donald's bracelet. She put on her own and went to join him in the Gallery of Dreams.

He sat on the naugahyde bench and worried the bracelet like it was a rosary, but his attention was on the paintings. If he noticed Sun come through the back door, he didn't show it. She stopped when she saw what was "playing" across the canvases. They had become screens for a documentary montage featuring none other than June and Julius Flower.

Sun felt sick looking at what was essentially a well-produced version of her parents' digital scrapbook—the secret one she had not been allowed to look at, was not supposed to know about. But she had known, she had looked—and now she knew that it had been intended, of course, like everything else in her life. Her parents had been in total control, and remained so. These documents and clips were part of the public record, after all. She might have found them on her own, piecemeal, one hurtful bit here, another humiliation later on. Instead, her parents had assembled the complete set of news items and video clips into a narrative, and trusted her to pry into it.

There was the initial modest splash of the Drs. Flower being welcomed to southern California in the back pages of the Oceanica Clinic newsletter. The scientists apparently came well recommended by an institute in Iceland and had received their degrees from the University of Stockholm.

The nature of their research was, "for the time being, undisclosed."

Then there were snippets and snapshots of the Flowers taken from various Clinic promotional materials.

There was a birth announcement for "Susan Flower."

And then came the first small news item about the couple going missing. They had left their one-year-old daughter in the care of work associates and gone off to a conference in Helsinki—at which they had never arrived and from which they did not return. Curiously, no family or old friends could be found to offer any clues or background on the couple at all. Neighbors and those in the professional community were left to speculate. The story worked its way to the front pages of the California papers after a month, went national for a week, and then was replaced by other scandals. Locally, the Clinic newsletter remarked from month to month that the Flowers were still missing, but their baby daughter was doing well in the care of Mr. and Mrs. Carson.

Mr. Carson's image appeared on the middle canvas—a young man wearing coveralls with the Clinic's insignia.

"Holy shit!" Donald leaned forward to get a better look.

"Not the same," Sun whispered from the shadows.

Donald was glad she was there. "You sure?" He turned to her.

"Yeah. All the people who help me are Carsons." Donald's jaw dropped. "Keep watching," Sun said before he could speak.

Young Carson's image was already fading out. Coming up in its place was the small back-page story of the Flowers' return exactly one year after their disappearance. Turned out they had been on an expedition to a remote jungle to study indigenous tribes untouched by western culture. The Carsons and two Clinic board members were aware of the plan. The Flowers hated to leave their baby daughter, but time was of the essence.

A week after the Clinic newsletter came out with the story, the Flowers' return monopolized a half-day of national news, after which the professors dropped out of the headlines and remained newsworthy only in academic and scientific circles. Their research was eventually published, but was discredited because they refused to reveal the identity or location of the group they had studied. They were discharged by the Clinic and began freelancing. Infrequent mentions of them in the journals increasingly cast them as "unconventional" and, ultimately, "crackpots." At last, according to a small item in *Psychiatric News*, "the once-notorious Nordic investigators of indigenous semiotics" had retired to grow apples in New England.

With the Flowers' bio-pic apparently complete, the montage of images flitting across the Gallery of Dreams canvases segued to the daughter. Donald followed the images eagerly, and, hearing Sun groan, reached out a hand to her. She shuffled over and plopped down next to him as her younger selves paraded dutifully before the camera. In the background, always the green lawn of one boarding school or another.

"I don't get it. I don't get it," Donald muttered.

"Me neither," Sun groaned.

"So much technology—I mean, what the hell? Is the bracelet activating it?!" He could feel his confusion bubbling up into anger again. He wanted to tear the paintings apart.

"And for what? To show us nothing! Baby pictures? College diplomas? News clippings? You don't need all *this* just for *that*! I wanna see what those things are really made of—"

"Wait! Something's happening." Sun took off her bracelet to examine it more closely. It was getting warm, glowing sightly. The canvases had gone dark when Donald lunged forward, stopping him in his tracks. He backed up and sat down again with Sun.

Credits began to roll in white on the darkened surface of the canvases. Only, they weren't credits. They were instructions to Sun and Donald:

PICK ALL OF THE APPLES AND MAKE A CIRCLE OF THEM AROUND THE TREE TRUNKS

STAND IN THE MIDDLE OF THE CIRCLE BETWEEN THE TWO TREES

DON'T FORGET YOUR TICKETS

TOUCH YOUR BRACELETS TOGETHER

COUNT TO TEN

BE BRAVE

WE LOVE YOU

MOM AND DAD

"Tickets? What could that mean?" Sun was perplexed but surprisingly calm.

"Tickets!" Donald reached into his pants pocket and found the parking tickets. "Well, damn. Check this out."

Two of the tickets were not from City Traffic. One had Donald's photo on it, and the sequence of symbols from his bracelet beneath. The other was printed with Sun's photo and symbols from her bracelet. They stood in the store with their heads bowed over the astonishing documents.

"What does it mean, Sun?" Donald whispered.

"Oh my gosh, Donald, I get it. I finally get it!" Sun felt an electric jolt run through her, felt herself come alive with the curiosity and drive that had always seemed lacking. Her hypnotic spell was finally broken, her mind released to discover the knowledge it had always held. She threw her arms around Donald and clutched him to her as if they had both just been saved from horrific catastrophe. Trembling, she put her lips close to his ear and shared the knowledge that her parents had stashed in her subconscious.

"My parents were not supposed to stay here so long. They were not supposed to have *me*! Not *here*! But their work is *working*. They're determined to stay. You and I will take their places."

Sun leaned back and looked into Donald's eyes. She saw no fear there, no confusion or anger. He said, nodding, "'They will be recycled into fuel. In time they will be used for transport.' I thought I heard those words when your father was telling me about the apples, even though that's not what he said out loud. So, your parents *are*—"

"*Not* space aliens, Donald. My parents are from the *future*. And *we* are going there!"

EPILOGUE

The fire that destroyed the Gallery of Dreams and convenience store burned so hot that no remains were found. The melted wreckage on the front curb was identified as Donald's car, parked unfortunately close to the hydrant. Another mangled heap in the back was Sun's. There was no question they had both been in the building. The neighbors mourned, but consoled themselves that the lovers had died together, probably in each other's arms.

Donald had always maintained he had no family, and no one showed up to prove him wrong. Everything from his apartment was donated to the local VA. A couple of military types came around and dropped hints about Donald having PTSD, but nobody who had known him was buying that Donald had set the blaze. The fire was declared an accident. The paintings were thought to be the likely cause, but as they'd been vaporized by the inferno, there as no way to determine exactly why they combusted.

June and Julius Flower came and surveyed the scene with a police escort. There were no mementos of their daughter to carry away, there was little left but ash. They stopped at Pantry Lane to see the Carsons, and the two couples went over to the Oasis Lounge. June and Julius sat grimly over their drinks and accepted condolences for half an hour.

The following spring the Flowers came out again and planted two little apple trees in the bulldozed lot, which, to everyone's astonishment, had sprouted a carpet of new grass. The neighborhood association was in the process of buying the land for a community garden and playground. They would name it Sun-Donald Park.

A couple of centuries later the entire block will have been consumed by nature, and Sun and Donald will be sitting under another generation of trees eating juicy apples. They will take turns reading from a journal left for Sun in a temporally secured deposit box. It will describe how, in her parents' time, before June and Julius traveled back, that same area was a toxic wasteland in which most forms of biological life were extinct. Humans had managed to save themselves, their bio-engineered food crops and, regrettably, their vermin. Achievements in materials technology, virtual environments and perceptual programming proved poor consolation for life in man-made, mechanized slums. The future had looked so bleak that no one thought of it except with terror, and all hopes and dreams were pinned on the past.

AFTER BABEL

by Prophetess Suomynona

BOOK III: Where were we?

After Babel, order doesn't mean anything.

BOOK II: "Because"

Everything is hyper-linked.

Everything . . . . All

Is . . . . Exists

Hyper . . . . Excessively

Linked . . . . Connected

BOOK 1: Turtles

INTERVIEWER: What do you mean by "consistency"?

OLDTIMER: Pick a way to do it, always do it that way.

INT: Why?

OTR: It makes things easier.

INT: How?

OTR: Like the alphabet—a to z—ABCDEFGHIJKLMNO-PQRSTUVWXYZ—consistent!

INT: Wow.

OTR: You want to find something that starts with G, look

after F; you want to find "turtle" you look near . . . ?
INT: I type it in. Here, look. Turtles. Everything I look for is always at the top of the list. Now *that's* consistent.
OTR: Sure, kid, sure.

BOOK ONE: Redundancy

See Book 1: Turtles
Keywords: *Turtle, turtle, Turtles, turtles*

BOOK I: You Are Here

Welcome to *After Babel*, the non-interactive, non-linear, non-sensical, post-poetry recollections of a lingering-on old gal. Just for kicks, y'know, 'cause they got me cooped up in this hitech cell with the Cloud on a steady dripdripdrip of pop culture and customized healthcare memos, and it's all crap. If civilization comes back one of these days, maybe this'll be a Book of the Bible. Right now, it's just a way to pass the time.

BOOK IV: Pink Bliss

The world has exploded
Everyone is armed, armoured
We stay home, interact via machine
Existence is spartan
We call it duck-tape decor
Even so, my face is full
of hydroponic watermelon
Could be worse.

BOOK VII: Language

AFTER BABEL FONTS SPEAK LOUDER THAN WORDS.

BOOK V: Shift Change

Nothing much to report:
Snookums did not want to eat her kibble.
Buddy was a good boy.
Zoe made up a song about her goldfish.
Marthe tried on 18 outfits
Took 40 selfies
Texted 16 friends
Tweeted 132 times.
The milk expired and sent a message.
The bulb in the bathroom will last 2 years at
Current rate of use.
4 bills were paid, 2 passwords were changed.
Do you want them?
        Got 'em already. Anything else?
Dammit, Rosie, don't you miss the old days?
        You mean when we only watched bad guys?
I'm sick of listening to people talk to their pets.
        Go home, Goldy. Blow off some steam. Give
        The spook who's spying on *you* something to do.

BOOK VI: Skunks

After they legalized pot
The big pot farms had trouble with skunks
The pot smelled so much like skunk
The skunks came around to check it out
For a while it was popular to trap the skunks
And remove their stink glands

Then let them back into the pot fields
The skunks dug a lot of holes and
Were bad for the crops
So then the farmers built big pens
At the entrances to the farms
To keep the skunks like mascots
These days you can't hardly go to a pot farm
Without seeing a pet skunk named "Bud"

BOOK VIII: Retaliation

The female majority in the U.S. Congress
In retaliation for legislation passed
By their male predecessors
Have not only stricken down all measures
Limiting access to birth control,
They have imposed a 72-hour waiting period
On heterosexual sex.
During this time the male is required to attend
Pregnancy prevention counseling. Further,
Intercourse may only take place
At specifically licensed facilities
Where the man can expect
To encounter aggressive protestors
And endure cruel taunts regarding his moral and
Physical fitness to perform the act
Before entering.
When women were asked
If this would be a sort of punishment
For them as well
69 percent said
Not really.

BOOK IX: Reparations

It's not all bad. Everyone's taken care of. The practical folks got around calling it Socialism by calling it Reparations. What's been holding you back? Native American kicked off the land? Migrant worker denied benefits? Descendant of slaves? Displaced farmer? War veteran? Woman? White man? (Well, what the heck.) No way to put a dollar value on lost opportunity, unpaid labor, absent assets. Wha'd'ya'say we just give you this housing credit, school enrollment, food card, health plan and transportation pass, for life, forever? Come on down to the employment office any time. The Reparations plan has created plenty of jobs, and we already know you'll be healthy and qualified. No obligation.

(Inside scoop: There is no obligation to accept a job under the Reparations plan, however, if you choose to opt out and sit home suckling off The Cloud—this is what I've heard, anyway—you will end up performing an administrative function for some agency or another. It works like this: Our use of electronics is constantly tracked in order to divine our habits. Then certain games and content are introduced that we are sure to return to again and again, and in doing so execute tasks or test systems for background programs. Thus, when it comes to myself and my desire to retain at least a semblance of autonomy, my madness is my method, if you get my drift.)

BOOK 2020: The Species Declines

I sat with my latte
looking hot
It was spring

I'd shaved my legs
They looked good
Stretched out not quite in the way
I would tuck them in the for the right young man
There were a few potentials by size and shape
I saw no faces
Bent to screens as they were
Thumbs tapping
I crossed my legs
Mother says it was a real nuisance
The way men wouldn't take their eyes off you
They were all horny as hell
And wanted to get into your panties
Or cop a feel
They'd look at you like they were hungry
It was powerful to be a good-looking woman
You could make a man come by crossing your legs . . .
I recrossed my legs
No one looked up
Their indifference made me want them more
I thought I was coming
But it was my phone vibrating
I had a message: "Nice"
Wth a zoomed-in snap of my pink lace panties
While I was uncrossing-recrossing
I jumped to my feet
A dude was coming to my table
Holding his I'm-a-dick phone
"Looking for company, babe?"
I grabbed his phone and dropped it in my latte
It was hot.

Book 11: Our Darkest Hour

After Blackout I hear the beeps and bloops of
defunct devices in the calls of birds
The buzz of insects reminds me
of the vibration that once asserted
—You're wanted—
even when the ringtone was silenced
The ringtone, the ringtone!
I dream that happy fragment of song that said
—You matter—
I matter!
The birds don't think so
They mock me
Their song is not for me
After Blackout the dark is absolute
No longer do I wade through stars on my way to bed
The stars are only in the sky now
outside my window
white pinpricks in the night
Where once the green and red
and gold and blue indicators
constellated indoors too
at knee and elbow height

Book XI: Lest We Forget

I took to carrying an empty rectangular frame just five inches by seven, because I no longer knew how to look at things firsthand. When I held up the frame and looked through, it was like seeing the world on a screen. And I could cope.

Book 13: Conspiracy Theory

It only took 30 years for everything on the internet to be garbage. In a nutshell: Click-through ad revenue dictated page search ranking. Crappy content on powerhouse platforms proliferated. Fact-based and first-person stuff fell by the wayside. Multinational corporations electrified the world, and everyone was wired into the Cloud. What a generous gesture! Reality didn't stand a chance. Nor humanity, while we ignored reality. Some say the "sunspots" that crashed the Cloud were a government plot to take back control of . . . Everything, I guess. In any case, it's better now, with Reparations and all. I'm grateful.

Book 010101: Modern Syndromes

1) Hearing phantom ringtones and computer chimes.
2) Seeing phantom indicator lights.
(An entire cottage industry has grown up around
"reading" these mysterious signals, similar to
fortunetelling by dream analysis.)
3) No one dreams anymore (that they will admit).
Because: "Human Enhancement" projects of past decades
appropriated all mental activity during sleep for
real-world sub-conscious problem-solving.
Discuss: Human evolution seemed to be moving toward
higher and more individual creative consciousness
but before such evolution could occur
we engineered ourselves into a hive.

Book 0

Babel = collapse of the hive
After Babel: we begin again

A MAN'S HOME IS HIS CASTLE

"Hand me that old CRT."

"The what?"

"The big clunky thing—be careful, it's a heavy MF."

"What's a MF? What's a CRT?"

"Nevermind, I'll get it. Stand here and hold this."

Jack, a pale, hulking eight-year-old, stepped over to the once-window and grabbed hold of the large microwave balanced in the glassless frame. The man, Blade, straightened up and mopped his forehead, scanning the cluttered floor of his dingy living room.

The last break-in had put Blade over the top. If he had to live in a fortress just to keep a roll of toilet paper in the john, so be it. All the glass on the first floor was long gone, anyway—and the daylight with it. Thick plastic and duct tape, then plywood and nails, had been used to cover the gaping windows. As it turned out, the building materials were more valuable than anything left in the house. He'd had one drink too many, slept a smidge too well, and everything got ripped off—literally ripped off! So that this morning the sun had peeked in on him like old times. But not for long. He only had this one window left to seal up.

The old electronic gadgets were truly useless. Some, like the CRT, had been slated for the dump long before the power went out. Now Blade was glad he'd never gotten around to hauling the stuff away. The whole history of the computer age lay strewn across his living room floor—short generations of audio, video and gaming equipment; printers, laptops, phones and screens of all sorts; speakers, boom-boxes and an assortment of CPUs. His sights were set on the biggest, baddest clunker of them all, an ancient 15", deep-backed monitor of the sort that used to pour radiation into the faces and chests of unsuspecting office workers. He picked his way over to it and considered whether to stand it upright on its puny plastic swivel base, or lay it on its back or face, or on one side or the other. He grabbed the thing and took a couple of well-placed strides back to Jack at the window.

"Keep it steady now," Blade instructed. Jack held the big microwave in place and twisted out of the way so Blade could slide the monitor on top. He set it in upright, monitor facing into the room. He'd have to fill in around the base. Plus, there was still a gap of a few inches at the top.

"Ya think you can hang onto them both?" Blade asked Jack.

"Aw yeah, sure." The big kid put one hand on each appliance, telling himself their names: *Microwave, CRT*. He always learned a lot when he came over to see Blade. "So, what's MF?" Jack asked again.

"Use your F'n imagination."

"Oh. Oh!" Jack tried not to imagine anything.

Blade messed around with several audio and video decks

before settling on an early-century combo. He would tilt the monitor down so the big back end raised up to make a reasonably level shelf, and slide the player in to fill most of the gap. He took the player over to the window and set it on the floor, then helped Jack get the monitor and microwave out of the frame and set them beside it. While Jack enjoyed having the sunshine stream over him, Blade ranged around the room gathering up cellphones and remote controls to wedge around the base of the monitor and fill any other gaps.

"What's all that?"

Jack's childish voice didn't synch up to his size. Blade tended to forget how young the boy was.

"This stuff? Well, these are remotes. You could push the buttons, and the TVs and radios and garage doors and stuff would work from wherever you were—you didn't have to go over to them to work them."

Jack huffed and looked frustrated, as he always did when the subject turned to that world of light and sound and speed he had never known—which it always did around grown-ups. Once upon a time the world had been full of amusements and magic devices, none of which was good for anything now but making Blade's "cement."

Jack watched as Blade grabbed up plastic parts—mostly from things he called "printers"—and put them into a giant grinder with a hand crank. Jack liked to turn the crank and watch all the stuff get smashed to bits. Blade, feeling vaguely guilty about his use of under-age labor, made Jack put on a pair of safety goggles before letting him crank.

The plastic shards were aimed into a bucket. When the bucket was two-thirds full, Blade was ready to stir in some water and a couple of scoops of cement powder. He was stingy with the powder, sprinkling it in like flour going into a cake batter until the consistency was just right. Getting enough water was becoming a problem. Today, the liquid in Blade's old coffee can was suspiciously yellow.

"Care to contribute?" he asked when Jack crinkled his nose. "No? Okay, here goes." He mixed up a bucketful of cement, wrinkling his nose too, to make Jack laugh. Then the two worked fast, stacking the appliances back in the window with thick gobs of cement in between, until all the gaps were filled and the room was so dark they could barely see what they were doing.

Blade moved a candle lamp closer to the grinder. He fed in the case from an electric pencil sharpener, a couple of calculators, and some other odds and ends. Jack held all the stuff in place in the window while the first batch of cement set up. Blade lugged the second bucketful around to the side of the house, leaving the front door open so Jack wouldn't be in the dark. No thieves were likely to come around in the middle of the day, while the neighborhood was bustling with people working on their houses.

Blade slapped his cement around the protruding back ends of the microwave oven, computer monitor and tape deck. The plastic chips sparkled in the sunlight. It would be even prettier with a coat of sealant over the whole thing. And impenetrable.

Blade had been able to swap a bag of his precious quik-krete for the polyurethane sealant at the community co-op. The co-op was set up in an old department store that had been looted and trashed right after the Outage. Blade was part of the local militia that quickly formed and eventually brought order to the community. They converted the store to a cooperative supply center, which worked entirely on the barter system. The second floor was made into a barracks for displaced women, children and old folks in need of protection. Those who could work were given jobs at the co-op. That's where Blade had met Jack and Jack's mother Pam.

Blade could tell that Pam was content with their little nook above the co-op. She felt safe there, where she was able to work and still be near her son. The two, Pam and Jack, naturally drew Blade's attention on his frequent stops for supplies—Pam because she looked nice, and Jack because of his size. To see more of them, Blade started showing up for some of the community games that had been cooked up to entertain the kids and help the grown-ups blow off steam.

The favorite activity of all age groups was TV Theater. The adults got together in groups to act out favorite episodes of their favorite TV shows for the kids. They quickly ran through the classics that everyone knew by heart—Lucy Ricardo trying to sell Vegameatavitamin, "The Trouble with Tribbles," the "Time Enough" episode from *Twilight Zone*. Then the productions began to take more effort. Team members huddled at lunch breaks to negotiate approximations of scenes and dialogue. Sometimes there were few words to work with, but everyone remembered how the show looked, how the characters spoke and interacted. The children could be kept busy with craft projects between weekly performances, like painting a colorful wall of cardboard doors for the set of *Laugh In* so that the adults could dress up in funny costumes and pop out to tell jokes they'd made up themselves.

Laugh In was such a hit they did it for a month, piecing together a little more each week. The grown-ups searched back through memories of days when they were only half-conscious, sprawled on bedroom floors and paying more or less attention to the Afternoon Classics channel while texting their friends. It was surprising, when they thought about it, how much the episodes had penetrated. More and more details surfaced. They found they knew those old series that had played in the background as well as they knew the new ones they'd hungered for each week and drank in with undivided attention.

On the last *Laugh In* night, Blade and Pam recreated the "Would you like a walnetto?" skit. Someone smaller should have played Arte Johnson's dirty old man, but Blade was not going to miss his chance to snuggle up to Pam on a park bench. He put on a long trenchcoat and bent his knees to make himself shorter. It gave him a funny waddle when he made his entrance. Pam did herself up like Ruth Buzzy's dowdy spinster as best she could, but the hairnet and baggy brown sweater and skirt did nothing to hide her beauty in Blade's eyes. Jack laughed up a storm when Blade scooted close to Pam on the bench and muttered lascivious-sounding nonsense, causing Pam to swat him with a big pocketbook.

Thanks to TV Theater, Pam had allowed Blade to befriend Jack. And thanks to Jack, she was letting Blade be her friend as well. Blade noticed that Pam had a way of returning what was given her in kind. She was friendly to those who were nice to her, prickly with those who were irritable, cool and professional with those who were businesslike, and snarly as a tiger with anyone who growled or grumped about her son. But as the weeks passed Blade felt that Pam was just herself with him, and he liked her more and more.

Blade had not made any romantic advances yet, apart from their duet on TV Theater. It was enough that Pam trusted him and appreciated his attention to Jack. For Pam, the fact that Blade would take Jack home with him for full days was a godsend. The child was enormous, and it was becoming a problem both at the co-op and upstairs in the barracks. Not that Jack was a problem, but others had a problem with him. Pam and Jack needed a real home. Blade was aware of that. That was the angle he was working.

Blade had never cared about courtship in the old days, during that life that seemed a million years away—when they'd had cold beer, animated action games, on-line poker, sports bars and those techno-clubs where decibles defeated conversation. There were Internet hotties you'd never find at the local bar, doing things local girls wouldn't ever do, couldn't even be asked. Those were the days. But they were gone gone gone now. Gone with the grid.

At least the chaos had passed, if not the crime. There were local governance committees and a global Good Samaritan network. There was "spot power"—rudimentary wind and solar converters that worked devices directly attached to them. Fire and steam energy, where there was something to burn. Water power, where there was water. Refinery fuels were pretty much used up, and batteries were treated like gold, but everyone had a lot of stuff—sufficient food and clothing or barterable items. Six years after the Outage, middle- and upper-class Americans were still living off their hoarded bulk goods. The co-op always had more than enough props, costumes and art supplies for TV Theater.

Blade was as well-set as anyone. All he needed now was a companion, and Pam was the one. Her mutant son had scared away the father, but Blade liked the boy. Sure, he seemed a little dense, but it wasn't the kid's fault he had been brought up in the dark ages. Everyone was freaked about how much Jack might grow. But Blade figured the world had turned upside-down already, and of all the weird shit that would be coming at them, having a giant for a son was not the thing to get hung up about. He had already seen a few advantages to it, and he refused to dwell on the many disadvantages and downright scary aspects of Jack's condition. That was all the more reason to reach out to Pam. He couldn't let her face that alone.

Blade figured if he could provide a secure home for Jack, Pam would come along. She wasn't crazy about him the way he was about her, but she didn't know him yet. Hell, he was only getting to know himself lately. He had a real creative streak, it turned out—besides the play-acting—a natural sense of mechanics and construction. He was good at making and fixing things, had to be, or he wouldn't've gotten by.

Blade finished up with the cement and took the long way around his "castle," admiring the sparkling fortifications at every ground floor window. Inside, he closed the door and let his eyes adjust. "How ya doin' in here?" he called to Jack.

"Cool. It's set."

"Hang the lamp from the old light fixture. Can you reach?"

Dumb question, the boy had a couple of inches on him already. Blade heard Jack clomping across the room, and a second later pale light filtered out to the hallway. Blade followed it into the living room, kicking the junk aside to reach Jack. They admired their handiwork. Where once there had been curtained windows, plastic-flecked cement sparkled, and lantern light bounced off the glass surfaces of old TV screens, monitors, and microwave and toaster oven doors.

"Cool, way cool," Jack breathed, feeling he was finally seeing all of these magical appliances lit up as they were meant to be.

"A few strategically placed glow-globes, and I think it'll be light enough to do stuff down here," Blade said. "We'll charge them every day up on the roof. And no one's gonna break in, that's for sure. The doors are the weakest link now, but I got bar locks on 'em all. Besides, who'd mess with the two of us?"

"The two of us?" Jack gave Blade a suspicious look, wondering if Blade would try to separate him from his mother, as so many others had tried to do.

"Come upstairs for a minute." Blade ignored Jack's wariness. He led the way and Jack followed. Turning right at the top of the stairs, they stepped into a tidy bedroom with an extra long single bed devised from two futons. "Ta da! The deluxe boy's room."

Jack swallowed hard, forcing down any stirrings of enthusiasm. He would not be tricked into abandoning his mother. "It's nice," he whispered.

He's just a little boy, Blade thought, realizing how stupid he was for not talking to Pam first. But here they were, on the tour. He patted Jack's back reassuringly. "I have something else to show you."

At the end of the hall Blade threw open the door of the master bedroom. Jack perked up immediately. He laughed out loud as he ran over to touch the wall of shiny disks. They were overlapped like scales on a fish, and had the same shimmering effect. Sunshine slanted in through the window opposite and bounced off the silvery fragments. There was no purpose to it that Jack could tell, since this room did not require fortification like the ones below. But maybe he was missing something. There was so much Jack didn't understand about grown-ups and their fairy tale devices.

"What was in them?" He felt smart for knowing that the mirror-like disks once held information, like a book—only now no one could open them.

"Nothing, everything. A lot of stuff I used to work with but have no use for now."

The glittering wall was a private joke on a guy who'd fastidiously created and backed up a million files—an accountant named Brad. Brad had blipped out with the electricity to be replaced by Blade. It was that, or cower in the dark until someone broke in and beat him up. The transformation began with Brad realizing he would have to defend himself and his property, preferably not with his bare hands. He found the sword and shield from his Ren Faire days. Brad hadn't scrimped on his toys back then. The sword, with its thirty-two-inch steel blade, had a true edge. The round shield known as a buckler was small but solid, an effective defense strapped to the left forearm. When Blade finally stepped outside into the fracas with his weaponry, people ran. Only a few weeks earlier, Brad's neighbors would've had a good laugh.

Jack sighed heavily. Grown-ups were always drifting off like that—saying something strange and then getting sad and quiet.

"Sorry, son. Don't mind me. The disks are just decoration now."

Had Blade really called him "son"? Jack was tongue-tied.

"Do you think your mom will like it?"

"My mom?"

"I'm gonna ask your mom to marry me, Jack. So you can both live here with me. I fixed up that room down the hall for you. I've got more disks. We could make another wall like this one."

"Me down the hall, and Mom here, with you?"

"If she'll have me."

"You'd be my Dad?"

He said it like it was too good to be true but still wondrous to imagine. Blade felt the same way. "I can't promise," he said, "but it would sure be cool, wouldn't it?"

"Yeah, cool! Way cool!" Remembering what his mother had taught him, Jack was careful not to hug Blade too hard.

YOU CAN ONLY GO BACK

You'd be surprised what you can learn on the SciNews channel if you pay attention. They broadcast university lectures, research review meetings and government-mandated stuff, all of which is really interesting if you don't try to watch it. The broadcasts are usually bare-bones and not much to look at, especially on a scratched-up hand-held where you can't hardly see anything. I like to sit in the cafe and listen through a headset while I work some puzzles and check out the scene.

The broadcast that changed my life was even less polished than most. A single camera aimed at the podium occasionally swung dizzyingly toward the audience and back again, or swept across the row of mucky-mucks who sat behind the speaker. Once it had zoomed in on Dr. Effinger and I'd gotten a good look at his face, I flipped the screen over to my games. It was easy enough to visualize the pleasantries on the dais and the fumbling around with a microphone set up in the aisle for questions from the audience. When Effinger finally got the go-ahead to start, he had me hooked from his opening line.

"Let me begin by saying that you can't go forward in time. The future isn't there to go to. Back and then back again is the only way you can go—

"Already a question? I've only gotten started. And this is a statement every Temporal Studies major has debated *ad nauseam* by their sophomore year—

"What's that? Oh, of course, Mrs. Sugarlake. For the sake of the audience at home. Forgive me, I'm not used to the lectures being broadcast.

"To answer the question, then— Sorry, what's that? Right, to pose the question, then. I didn't let the fellow ask it, but I knew what it would be. I'd only made one statement: 'You can't go forward in time; there is no future to go to.' And one pressing question derives from this: But once you go *back* in time, and your present becomes your *future*, does that existence cease to be? Poof—it never happened?

"That *was* going to be your question wasn't it? Something like that? Yes, I thought so.

"There are two ways to look at it. You could say that your *present* from which you traveled back in time will become your *past* just like any other experience, part of a sequence of events that proceeded to a certain point. To *return* to the point at which you left would mean going *back* to a moment in your *past*. You see? From the vantage of the past you've traveled to, returning to where you started will *seem* like you are going forward, to the future, which I have said is impossible. But logically, the moment perceived as the *now* of your departure has come and gone, and any return involves actually traveling *back* to *your past*. So, it is theoretically possible to travel to the past, then return to the point at which you left and resume your life sequence from there, and nothing will have gone Poof.

"Logic is lovely, isn't it? There is logic and then there is logic. Another, also logical way to look at this, is to suppose that when you visit the past you will inevitably influence a chain of events that will result in alterations of the circumstances that led to the moment when you set forth. At that point, I fear you have lost your past, your present *and* your future, from the perspective of the original sequence of events that make up your memories. Possibly you will lose the memories themselves—but that is in the realm of psychology and not physics—

"What's that? Oh, hecklers, now! I do apologize to the remote audience. Everyone here has been round and round on this already. They grow impatient. So let's let one of them ask and answer the next obvious question, and see if he can do so any better than I. Go ahead, young man. Yes, you, who's so impatient, you in the ridiculous orange vest."

At this, I had to pause my game and screen over to the broadcast. A slight, blond man was fidgeting with the mic stand. His vest was florescent orange, appropriate for road work or a deer hunt, and far too large for him.

"Ehem, uhm, alright— Mic on? Alright, the question: Are you saying that the future—that is, the present—once you've left it for the past—that *this* time-place ceases to exist when *anyone* goes back in time? Everyone in it just blips out? Along with everything *in between* this moment and the time you go to in the past? That unless the time traveler has absolutely *zero* influence on the past, which is mathematically impossible, his going back will cause, like, a reboot of the whole timeline?"

"Indeed. Does traveling to the past reboot the timeline? Well asked, once you got to it. Now, what is the answer?"

"Ehem. Right. The answer."

"For the viewing audience, now. So if you were planning on using the term *local field* we'll expect an explanation."

"Right, right. Local field. I think I can do without that. Right. Here we go: Imagine time is a pond. The time traveler is a fish. Let's just say that a bird comes along and plucks that fish out of the water, flies some distance away, and drops him back into the pond. We won't worry about which direction the bird flies right now, just that it scooped up this person, transported him some distance, and dropped him.

"Everyone got that? You can see in your mind's eye that there is a disturbance of the water at both points—where the fish leaves the pond, and where it is dropped back in—as evidenced by ripples radiating outward from the points of disturbance on the surface of the water. Yet, in the scope of the *entire* pond, the ripples are mild and subside within a fairly short distance. The disturbances in the water have occurred at a distance from one another. Plus, they have not been simultaneous—some time elapsed between the fish being plucked out and dropped back in. The outward rings of ripples never converge on each other, and have no superficial effect on a good percentage of the pond. Most of the pond is unaffected by the relocation of the fish, in the same way that the overall structure of time does not collapse when a person travels from one point to another. Plus, even on the local level, the ripples can be minimized—to extend the metaphor—by keeping the fish small, removing it with precision, and dropping it from a short distance.

"Uhm. That's all, I think. Thank you."

"Thank you, young man. Clever, isn't he? Clever, but clear as mud. The poor befuddled people out there simply want to know if they are going to blip out of existence the minute one of our meddling Historians hops back in time to see his favorite baseball game. Anyone?

"Ah, yes. Mrs. Sugarlake would like to address this point. Mrs. Sugarlake is Director of the Temporal Education Taskforce, which is sponsoring this public broadcast. Mrs. S., do take the podium and tell us why we needn't worry about Temporal Exploration unraveling the fabric of time. I think it would be good for my know-it-all students to hear this put into civic terms. Here you go. I'll move over there, you stand right here and give everyone's eyeballs some relief. I'm really getting off easy today, aren't I?"

I stayed with the video long enough to get a look at the

lovely Mrs. Sugarlake. She navigated a row of well-creased masculine knees, arrived at the podium, and did a little do-si-do with the professor. Once the camera had shown me her dazzling smile, I clicked back to my game and continued to listen:

"Actually, I think we've scuttled your teaching plan quite terribly, Dr. Effinger, and you're being a very good sport about it. Thank you, and thank you all for such lively participation. Let me first of all emphasize that no one will be 'blipping out of existence' on account of any Temporal Exploration activities. While I know it is here used in jest, this is exactly the sort of alarmist, reactionary language and fear-mongering I have been appointed to defuse. I'll leave the technical explanations to Dr. Effinger, because we're not saying things won't change. It is always expected, in fact intended, that research and the knowledge it brings leads to change—for the better. We call that Progress. That's right. Undertaken correctly, Temporal Exploration of history will not undo our present times—far from it. It will enhance them. We are using Temporal Exploration to secure a more peaceful, prosperous future. Thank you."

"Don't tell me that's all, Mrs. Sugarlake? You're throwing it back to me so soon? I thought you would explain what it means to undertake TE 'correctly.' Don't you want to expand on that?"

"Oh, well, of course. If you like. Just let me have a word with Admiral Klunkel. Mustn't give away any classified information, you know."

"Ah, the complications of live broadcast. Looks like I'm back in the hot seat. So be it. Let us return to ripples. Viewers, don't get too many ideas about the orange-vested one's brilliance. We use the pond-and-ripples metaphor quite a lot in this discipline. It's useful, as the gentleman indicated, for just about all aspects of time travel but the directional issue, which we'll get to in a future lecture—provided there *is* a future— Just kidding, Mrs. S., must inject a little humor here and there, don't you think?

"Getting back to the ripples: The fish is dropped into the water. Say it's not even a fish, just a pebble. It's dropped into the water and then sinks, initiating no movement of its own. We have the ripples, mild ones if it is a small pebble dropped from a short distance, but even if it's a large stone dropped from a high flying pterodactyl and makes a tremendous splash, the ripples will eventually diminish. The water's surface will again be calm and even, subject to other influences but no longer the rock's.

"Still, our pebble or rock displaces water all the way down to the bottom of the pond. Its influence is not just on the surface and not just local. Once a single molecule shifts, any number of others might. What is the impact on the bottom of the pond? Or the distant shore? There are always repercussions. This is the very essence of Time—one thing following another. Every action has an equal and opposite reaction, and in the case of time travel these reactions go on forever. This is why Temporal Exploration must be undertaken with the utmost caution, and *is*— As Mrs.

Sugarlake will now explain? Ah, no, it will be the distinguished Admiral Klunkel himself—

I screened over in time to see the beribboned Admiral appropriating the professor's spot at the podium. The mic caught every word:

"We are getting everyone into the act today, aren't we? But I have to say, Mrs. Sugarlake looked a lot better on the dais than you do, Klunkel."

"Backatchya, Effy. You're no help sometimes, you know that?"

"Then by all means, set the record straight. I'm only trying to keep this on a scientific level."

"And we appreciate that. We certainly do."

The admiral shouldered the scientist out of the way and turned to the camera.

"But what people need to know is that you and me and Mrs. Sugarlake and her committee and your students and future Historians of the past, are fully, and I mean fully, cognizant of all the pitfalls of time travel and are doing absolutely everything to avoid them. We don't need to shine a light down every hole just to tell the folks we'll be sure to keep our foot out of it. We know our limits. And I want to go back to what the fellow said about picking out the right fish, in the right way, and dropping it back in the right place from the right distance so we minimize the ripples. The fish is the time traveler, see? And we at

Temporal Security have very strict guidelines about who goes where, when. Get it? I'm not free to reveal all the details. I'll just say that we only go where we know where we're going, first of all, and that's why we only go *back* in time. And we only send folks who know everything about the time-place they're going to, and that's why we only send *Historians*. And we do everything we can to cause as few ripples as possible, and that's why we have a *Temporal Code of Conduct* that everyone in this unit swears to uphold under penalty of death. Got that?

"Your timeline is safe with us. That's all I have to say."

"Ohhh-kay then. Mrs. Sugarlake? Anything to add? I believe Admiral Klunkel's mention of 'future Historians of the past' could use some clarification. We may have some potential Temporal Explorers right here in the audience, after all, and they'll want to know what they're in for— Oh, you want *me* to explain? Very well, with the Admiral's permission—

"Good. Now, with apologies to my students, I'll return to the fish in the pond. I promise we'll get to Chapter Six, Temporal Increments, in the next lecture.

"So, the fish makes waves when it's dropped into the pond, but also, remember, when it is plucked from the pond. Our time travelers are all dedicated Historians, eminently qualified to enter and blend into the past, and pledged to a strict code of honor concerning historical events. Historians are also by nature bookish and prone to slip away on research trips, which reduces the impact of their disappearance from their home locale. It is understood that time travel is possible without unraveling time, but you do have to watch out for the ripples on both ends. The Historian goes back and only back to a past he knows thoroughly. Before he becomes entrenched enough to have an impact on the local field, or for his inevitable disappearance to disturb the local field, he goes back again."

"Excuse me, sir. You used the term 'local field'—I thought we were going to avoid that."

"You again, Orange Vest. I said *you* were to *explain* it if you used it, and you did an admirable job of avoiding the challenge. Would you care to explain it now?"

"It's just the piece of the pond you're in at any moment, all of Time being the pond."

"Succinctly stated. Thank you. As I was saying. The Historian goes back. He or she inhabits a new local field and makes every effort not to make waves. Keeping the duration of the visit short helps. Also being inconspicuous, so that when he or she leaves to make the next jump to the past, there will be few ripples. And so, our Historians have multiple past lives, you might say. They research a time thoroughly and go to it, where they assume the role of Historian again, to research the next station in the past. The travels are not random. There is a plan and a purpose. Itineraries and contingency plans are filed with the Temporal Security Administration. Once in motion, our Temporal Historians never stay put, never return to their original time or try to communicate with us directly—which alleviates any concern for whether we are here or not, I might add—except that Mrs. Sugarlake and Admiral Klunkel are glowering at me.

"Anyway. Hmmm. Who would like to ask the next obvious question, on behalf of the viewing audience? Ah, Jaquie, a familiar face. Have at it."

"Thank you, sir. The next question must be: Why? If the Historians go back in time and are never seen again or have any contact with us, and if they are sworn not to 'make waves,' as you say, and if a misstep really could unravel the timeline as we know it, why are they going back at all? Isn't it a great risk to *us*, for the sake of fulfilling *their* curiosity? And it sounds like a dangerous and frightening life for the Historian—never permitted to really settle down. And I have to ask another question if you don't mind, sir: How do the Historians age? When they go back in time and start living forward again, only to go back again, et cetera, what is the effect on their physical systems? I suppose we will never know, will we? What's the point of the research if we can never see the results?"

"That is three or four too many questions. I'll stick to the essential nut of it: 'Why?' Jaquie asks. What is the point to all of this leaping back never to be seen or heard from again?

"The reason is the ripples. Yes, the reason to be exceedingly cautious in traveling time is the very reason to do it. The pebble has an effect under the water too, remember. Molecules shift, even at extreme distance from the original disturbance. Might the careful Historian leave a meaningful footprint for us, whether or not we are aware of the effect? Perhaps it will be an attitude, a new way of looking at history, or even a more perceptive record *of* history. Molecules knock against each other. An enlightened thought percolates both forward *and* back in time.

"Well, look at that. Even my advanced students are getting interested now. I see a question on the tip of your tongue, Spalding. Let's have it."

"Sir, it seems like you're saying that the history we know is not all written by people of the past, that Historians of the future may have gone back and added to it."

"That *is* what I'm saying. But hold your gasps for this next revelation— Now don't get your knickers in a knot, Admiral. I'm certain this is on the approved outline. Mrs. Sugarlake, please show the Admiral item, uh, IIIA on the outline. That's all I'm getting into, I promise— Okay?

"Good. Oh drat, now I forgot where I was— Let's see, IIIA— Right. Here we go. Certainly, Historians of the future helped write our histories of the past. The how-we-know part is classified. But the fact, rather a reassuring one, I think, that *can* be shared—we only share reassuring facts, right, Mrs. Sugarlake? —is that the means to travel through time was itself given to us by people of the future, so subtly that at first we thought we were getting it ourselves. *They* created the precedent by which we only go back. Though *we* feel we have proved mathematically that it is possible to travel time forward, we have no intention of trying it. Because, if the rules of time travel indeed come to us from the future, we must assume their authors know something about the dangers of breaking them that we don't know. Although we certainly can *imagine* the worst, thus requiring Mrs. Sugarlake's department.

"Well, speaking of time, looks like ours is up. Let me sum up, with my tongue only lightly in my cheek, by pointing out that our being here today, in satisfactory continuity from all the days before, is all the proof we need that time travel to the past can be, *and has been*, undertaken safely.

"Now we will have a parting word from Mrs. Sugarlake. Class, stay behind, please, so we can go over the assignment. Mrs. Sugarlake—"

"I just want to thank Professor Effinger, and also Admiral Klunkel. Come up and stand with us for a photo, won't you, Admiral? And my thanks to our students here as well as our remote audience. Please watch for upcoming lectures on *New Frontiers in Time*.

"Smile, gentlemen."

"Crock of shit."

"Someone cut that mic!"

"This live broadcast has been brought to you by the Temporal Education Taskforce on behalf of the Temporal Security Administration. Dr. Herman H. Effinger is Department Chair of Temporal Studies at the National Sciences Academy, and author of the book, *No Time Like the Present*. We now return to your regularly scheduled programming."

"Well, I'll be a—" I held the Private Wireless over my head and called out, "Hey, anyone just catch this thing on SciNews?!"

What did I expect? The ones who weren't ignoring me jeered back, "Shut up, you geek!" "Use the cafe ticker, bonehead!" and words to that effect.

It's true I could've beamed a ticker message to anyone in the cafe who was looking at a PW, which was just about everyone. But I was too blown away by what I'd just seen to mess with messaging. And I bet if there *had* been someone else in there watching SciNews, they'd've been right with me, ready for some face talk. But no. Everyone was on the remote make—using the cafe system so they could get on the dating lines or shop for porn or maybe just trade stamps without giving out their real identities. And this place calls itself The Think Tank. Yeah right. My bad.

So I turned in the PW, got some tokens for the unused time, and went to the Barbershop. That's a club for old farts. Bunch of decrepit dudes sitting around all watching the same monitor, drinking beer and not caring one damn about their potbellies, and talking to each other. I'm not allowed to talk because I'm not old enough to be a member of the club, but I can go hang out as long as I keep my mouth shut and let Bonsai cut my hair once a month whether it needs it or not. It's Bonsai's place. Marketing genius, that guy. Doesn't take a drop, but makes a wad selling brewskies to his buddies. They're happy to shell out for it, makes up for the haircuts they don't get anymore now that they're bald. Old Bonsai makes up in short what he lacks in fat. Stands on a crate to cut your hair, and is like to get blown away in a strong wind, but he is smart. And not half bad with a shears.

Sure enough, the fellows at the Barbershop had caught the SciNews broadcast. The monitor was still tuned to the station but the sound was down. The old men paid no attention to the half-naked actors playing out a simulation of prehistoric fertility rites. Bonsai says there's actually a clause in the Broadcast Security Administration rulebook about always airing something arousing and sexually graphic after a broadcast that might "distress the citizenry," and always airing something scary and violent after any program that's "excessively spiritually uplifting." I suppose he could be making it up, but since we started paying attention, it seems like they really do run it that way. Bonsai knows a hell of a lot about everything.

Anyway, it was a little bit harder for me to be as casual about those brown titties dancing around all over the big screen, so I put my back to it and made myself listen to what the guys were saying about Effinger's lecture. It didn't surprise me that Bonsai was keeping mum on this one. He's a cagey dude. He was letting his good buddy Sherm do all the talking, as usual, while nodding now and then and looking a little preoccupied.

Sherm was saying: "Looks like they're still worried about Quinn Fletcher. Remember that nutcase? He was the darling of the temporal science crowd until he started peddling the 'future jump.' The kids loved it. Everyone was into it for a while, while it was all hypothetical. But he started pushing for research money. New protocols. He had students lining up to try it out. I think it was this Effinger himself who dubbed Fletcher the Time Bomb, said he would be sending the coeds on a suicide mission, and maybe risking 'life as we know it.'"

"I don't get it, Sherm," the dude they called Toad croaked. "Goin' *back* seems more dangerous. Like the man said—*Poof!*—timeline's zapped. Goin' forward—what's to screw up?"

We all leaned in to hear what Sherm would say. Temporal stuff was his specialty.

"You gotta think of time as cumulative. That is, time is made of events and events are cumulative. In order to travel through time—or at least navigate—you gotta be aware of events. You can learn about the events of the past, like the Historians do—use them like points on a map. Events of the future, our future, are unknown. Some events can be predicted—like the seasons or movements of the planets. But unexpected natural or man-made disasters might alter even that. And the human element is way harder to predict. Now, a Historian working his way back to the past could drop some hints about the future, or give instructions flat out. Effinger kind of implied that has happened. So maybe you could take that information and try to jump forward—quick, before that future changes on account of the ones who traveled back in time to tell you. Maybe Fletcher thought he had an inside track on that. But it can't work that way. Any future is only an accumulation of events from the past, any of which might play out differently if any of which have been altered by time travelers. In *theory*, sure, one might travel to the future, but it would always be an unknown, so how do you know where you're going?

"Now here's another puzzle: A traveler from the *present* arriving in the *future* will not have participated in intervening events. He was not part of that span of skipped-over time. So the future he goes to isn't *his* future—it's his present, but not his future. What are the implications for the span of years in which the time traveler was *nowhere*? Going *back*, one always continues to be in the world, to exist, because the accumulation of events that is the past always belongs to everyone—those events are done, if sometimes done over. And everything in the present results from those events. The future doesn't happen until everything else has happened first."

By this time the old men were groaning and holding their heads. "Stop already," "You're giving me a headache," "Such a *mishegas*," they complained, and looked to Bonsai to back them up.

But all Bonsai said was, "I wonder why he was wearing that orange vest."

That puzzled everyone, and they all reached for their mugs and took a swig as one, trying to rinse tangled thoughts from their ancient brains. Pretty soon after that Sherm left in a mild huff. These guys were so low on testosterone they couldn't hardly get insulted or mad about anything anymore. They just got tired. One by one the others shuffled out, until it was just me and Bonsai.

I opened my mouth, but before I could speak he said, "Shut up, kid," and went back to washing out beer mugs in the shampoo sink. I closed my mouth. He hadn't said, "get lost," so I kept my perch in the third swivel chair and tried to digest everything I had just heard.

And then "Orange Vest" walked in. I almost fell off the chair, but Bonsai seemed to be expecting him. The guy looked a lot older than he had in the broadcast, on my three-inch PW screen. Fine lines patterned his waxy face, and his hair was old-man white, not sun-bleached blond. Slight of build like Bonsai, he had taken off the orange vest and held it at his side like it was heavy and weighing him down.

"I'm beat," he said, plopping down on the tattered couch the old men had so recently occupied. "Thought they'd never leave." He let the vest drop to the floor and gave me a dirty look. "I guess *you* never do."

I opened my mouth to apologize, but Bonsai said, "He ain't allowed to speak in here," and I swallowed my tongue again.

"Since when are you so big on rules?" Orange Vest asked, kind of nasty.

"Since I make my own," Bonsai snarled back.

"You're a shit, but it's still good to see you."

"You the one who put that bee in Fletcher's bonnet? Seems like you've been breaking a few rules yourself."

"Fletcher's all washed up here. It's my fault, but I needed some help. Couldn't go through the usual channels. I'm taking him back with me. That is, I'm taking him forward. Get him out of the way here. Get him to a future that has a future, if you know what I mean."

"Screw that. Whatever you do up ahead is not my problem, unless you make one for me. You here to screw me up? Setting me up for a little 'accident'?"

"Naa, shit. What do I care? So you get yourself a barbershop and live out a cushy life after just a few jumps. You're not the first to ditch the mission, and you won't be the last. If this kid weren't sittin' here, I'd say no harm done. As it is," here he gave me a look that froze the blood in my veins, "he better be a viable recruit or we're gonna have a *couple* accidents."

"I got a plan for him, don't worry. So, what's with the vest?"

"Picked it up on my travels. Full of gear from up ahead. Found it in a cave dwelling. Can you beat that? Bunch of bones and this thing. Bears didn't like the taste of it, evidently."

"You've been that far back?" Bonsai had a look on his face I had never seen before—a look of respect.

"I've been all the way back to the *beginning*, bro," the oldest of old men said wearily. "They never mentioned that in the Code, did they? I figure at that point, we're all improvising. So, I turned around and started jumping forward. Ended up a damn TE maid. Folks up ahead are getting sloppy, really need a talking to. I don't know how far I'll get, but *someone's* gonna see that Effinger broadcast *someday* and recognize this thing," he kicked the high-tech garment at his feet, "and maybe get a clue."

"The talk itself was too early," Bonsai muttered, shaking his head. He'd taken a seat in one of the swivel chairs. "You worried about what you'll find up ahead?"

"Naa, just *where* I'll find it. Like you said, things're speeding up. Gotta be careful I don't jump too far."

"Would it help if I went back to work? Back and back again, as the professor says?"

"Naa. You're too much of a fixture here now. You'd leave a hole. *Like the perfesser says*. Better send this one in your place."

He nodded my way, and my frozen blood turned into hot lava. I realized this had been Bonsai's plan for me right along.

Orange Vest noticed me sweating and said, "It ain't so

bad. You know you're curious. You got the history bug. I can tell. Or you wouldn't be hanging around *this* place."

I wanted to tell him he was right. That I would go. That I *had* to go, now that I knew it was possible. But when I opened my mouth, Bonsai said, "Shut up, kid. Learning to keep your mouth shut is the first lesson." Then he got up and fished around in a cupboard until he found a tattered paperback. He tossed it into my lap.

It was a *Code of Temporal Conduct*—undated. I spent the rest of the evening paging through it, keeping my mouth shut and my ears open, while two pebbles talked about the pond late into the night.

□ □ □

About Amador Publishers

In 1986, Harry Willson and Adela Amador founded Amador Publishers, dedicating their press to "peace, equality, respect for all cultures and preservation of the biosphere." They quickly set about fulfilling their mission. In addition to publishing Harry's books, the press took on authors of Southwest and literary fiction, including Michael H. Thomas, David L. Condit, Tim MacCurdy, Michelle Miller Allen, and Zelda Leah Gatuskin. Adela gained notoriety in her own right with her recipe books, New Mexico *cuentos*, and a 13-year stint as the author of the "Southwest Flavor" column in *New Mexico Magazine*.

The press gained national and international recognition with "the world's first anti-smoking novel" by Arthur L. Hoffman, the fiction works of acclaimed literary scholar Gene H. Bell-Villada, and the WWII memoirs and fiction of Eva and Manfred Krutein.

Recent titles from Amador Publishers include two significant works by author-activist Donald Gutierrez, *Feeling the Unthinkable: Essays on Social Justice* and *The Holiness of the Real: The Short Verse of Kenneth Rexroth*; the collected poems of Robin Matthews, *Another Spring*; and *From Fear To Love: My Journey Beyond Christianity*, Harry Willson's philosophical memoir, edited by Zelda Leah Gatuskin.

www.ingramcontent.com/pod-product-compliance
Lightning Source LLC
Chambersburg PA
CBHW051551280626
47162CB00021B/1676